Slipping in Sin

Sarah E. Jamison

This book is a work of fiction. Names, characters, places and incidents either are products of the author's imagination or are used fictitiously. Any resemblance to actual events or locales or persons, living or deceased, is entirely coincidental.

ISBN 978-0-984-04160-2

Published by: Metamorphosis Publications

Newtown Square PA

Cover layout/design by Designs by SheShe
Editors: Carla Dean

Printed in the United States of America

Contact for comments or to order books:

www.johnsonpublications.biz

ЖDedicationЖ

This dedication goes out to everyone that helped make this book successful. I want to thank the one and only true and living, who made the heaven and earth and everything in it. I want to thank God for Jesus. John 3:16: *For God so loved the world that he gave his only begotten son, that whosoever believeth in him should not perish, but have everlasting life.*

I want to thank God for inspiring me with his Holy Spirit, which lives in me. HE leads and guides me. If it wasn't for his Holy Spirit, I couldn't have written a single word.

I want to thank God for the following:

My mother who gives me that smile that speaks. I'm proud of how God is using you. You cherished my first book, *Echoes From Heaven*, and blessed me when I saw you one day at a family gathering by pulling my book out to show to someone. You then took it and held it to your heart. I'm glad God blessed me with you to be here to enjoy this book's ministry with me.

I thank God for my brothers and sisters whom I love so much. For my uncles, aunts, cousins, nieces, nephews, in-laws, and dear friends whom I also love dearly.

I thank God for our children, Tanya and Steve (our son-in-law), Wilber Jr., Christian, and Dominique. You have always been good, disciplined children. You have always been supportive and show love to your father and me. Also, I thank God for our four grandchildren: Kenya, Shanyra, Ta'Mya, and Na'hari. Four jewels that He has given us. We love you, and you love us.

I thank God for my publisher, who is also my niece, Latia Johnson, and her husband Ron. I thank God for all the good advice and teaching that he gives me through you. I thank God for the patience that he has given to you for me and me for you, because this book was a piece of work. I had everything all over the place, but Latia, you helped me get it all together.

I thank God for Evangelist Pauline Rice, Mrs. Chequeta Simmons and Mrs. Diane Roberts, who are always praying and encouraging me. I thank God for all of my co-workers who support and encourage me in my book ministry. I thank God for Aleesha Hale, my future daughter-in-law, and my co-worker, Mrs. Danny Ell, for helping me with some of my settings in this book. I thank God for one of my angels that he has sent to me on my job. When I need help concerning my computer or anything else, Mrs. Beth Becker is right there with a genuine smile followed by genuine help. I thank God for all three of these last sisters that I mentioned because they helped me when I was in desperate need of help.

ℰ𝒪 *Thank You* ℬ

I thank God for Vision of Missions Tabernacle Church, Apostle Van Zane, and Co-Pastor Phyliss E. Moore, and God's Vision Ministry Inc., Pastor Thomas Bryant, and Co-Pastor Kathryn Bryan. Both of these churches support me to the fullest, financially and spiritually with many prayers. I call them my spiritual fans.

I save the best for last, but not least. I thank God for my husband, Will, who shows how proud he is of me in his own quiet, sensitive, loving way. I can't imagine living without him. We have been together since I was sixteen years old. We are happy and still in love. We been through many trials and tribulations, but God helped us through each one that came our way and will continue to help us. I thank God for all of the love and support he has given me through all of these people.

Forward

We go through so much--good and bad--in our lives, but the good outweighs the bad every time. God comes to you in this short novel to demonstrate that good is a reality and so is bad. Reading this book, you will agree that it is truly a reality of what is happening in some people's lives today!

When evil and trouble comes our way, we have to be strong and know that we can hang in there until it passes. On the same note, we have to confess to ourselves that we need help.

We have to understand that we can't endure evilness that comes our way by ourselves. Sometimes we experience what seems like a minute, but it's a season when things are going fine in our lives. Then it seems like another minute, but it is another season when things are going bad in our lives. At times, seasons change so fast, and we are in a state of wonder. We wonder what happened and how did I get in this bad state of mind. One minute, we're praising God for what he is doing for us, and the next minute, we're questioning God on what he is doing or allowing to happen to us. God allows some things to happen to us to build us up, for God knows what is best for us. We make mistakes, but God never make mistakes.

When you read this book, you will experience bad times that will make you sad and good times that will bring you joy. God shows us the good and the bad, because God is not a God that will leave us in the darkness or have you thinking that life is going to be sweet and good all the time. Yet, He will show us how he will always be with us despite what we go through in life, and that he will step into situations in our life if we trust him and only him, because he is a jealous God. He will let no devil or no one get the glory of those whom he calls ordained, anointed, and appointed to use for his glory!

Go ahead. Read it for yourself! Enjoy!

Intro

Robert Allen Love was a medium-build, handsome, dark brown-skinned, young man. He was in extremely good shape, with broad shoulders, a buff chest, muscular arms, and a trimmed waist. He was everything a woman would dream of having in a man, and his personality fit his body––banging.

He was conservative, quiet, and shy. He didn't lust after or try to play on women. He was raised up in church with Godly principles by both of his parents, Theodore and Gloria Love. As he got older and remembered the things he was taught, two things kept coming to his mind: Proverbs 18:22 - Who so findeth a wife findeth a good thing, and obtaineth favour of the Lord, and Proverbs 31:10-31, the teachings of the qualities of a wife. He was taught if a woman pushes herself on you, then she is not the kind of woman you should want to marry.

Robert had gone to college, received his Master's degree in Business Management, and was now a manager at the National Penn Bank in Philadelphia. At the age of twenty-one, Robert still lived with his parents due to the fact that every time he planned to move out, his father would get sick. So, to help his mother care for his father during his sickness, he just remained at home with them.

Robert was twenty-two years old when his father died due to his heath failing. His father was sixty years of age at the time of his death. Nine months later, Robert's mother had a heart attack. She was also sixty years old when she passed. It's believed that she died of a broken heart from losing her husband, choosing to join her husband in death than be without him in life. With him being an only child, his parents had left him the house, plenty of money, and everything else they had. Robert didn't need for anything. Accepting to be led by God, whom he depended on to help him through this rough time of his life, he continued going to church in order to gain the strength and support he needed to get him through one day at a time.

A year later, on one bright, sunny, but cold Sunday morning in October, Robert went to church as usual. The message for the day was *This is Your Day* taken from

Psalms 118:24. After the word was given, Pastor Brian O'Neil opened the floor for Discipleship. "Is there one who has heard God's word and will come to give God thanks for this day he has blessed you with to rejoice in?" Pastor O'Neil said to the congregation. "Will you come and ask Jesus to come into your heart to lead and guide you every day from this day forth? Will you come and let this be your day?"

Three young men began walking up to the front of the altar and following behind them were two young women. As the five individuals stood at the front of the church, Robert Allen Love's eyes widened with tears of joy. *Oh my God,* Robert thought to himself. *He that findeth a wife findeth a good thing. God, I have been looking and waiting Sunday after Sunday, and this is my day. Oh God, thank you. I've found my wife. Thank you, God!* He clearly was experiencing love at first sight!

Rosetta Ann Mathis was a beautiful young lady. Her skin was a pretty light brown complexion and had a glow to it. She didn't need to even think of wearing makeup. Her hair was jet black and styled into a short Halle Berry cut. Standing at 6'5", her measurements could be compared to the curviness of an hourglass––38-24-36.

She had completed college, obtained her Master of Arts in Education, and was a teacher in the Philadelphia public school system.

This day, she came to church with one thing on her mind, and it wasn't Jesus. She was tired of being alone, and she had heard if you want a good man, you need to go to church. Well, Rosetta received a double blessing that day. She received Jesus to lead and guide her new life with her new friend, Robert.

After the service was over, Robert went over and introduced himself to the sister who he had his eyes fixated on during the pastor's entire sermon. With his hand extended to shake hers, he introduced himself.

"Hello, my name is Robert Love. Welcome to Fishers of God Baptist Church," he said, welcoming her to the church.

"Thank you," Rosetta responded, while looking into in his eyes as thoughts rushed through her head. *Wow! He's so fine and muscular. I hope he'll ask for my name. How can it be possible for me to love him already and I don't even know him yet? Oh, I could just melt in his arms.*

Just as she had hoped, Robert asked, "What's your name?"

"My name is Rosetta Ann Mathis," she replied, stating her whole name.

"I love your name. It matches you, because you are pretty as a rose," he complimented. "Did you come with someone or do you have someone coming to pick you up?"

This was Robert's opportunity to see if she had a male friend or husband.

"No," Rosetta replied. "I don't have anybody in my life but God and me."

That was music to Robert's ears. "Well, may I have the pleasure of taking you home?"

She couldn't answer fast enough, but trying to be cool, she calmly said, "I would love for you to take me home."

So, they walked to the church door. After Robert opened it, he followed behind her as she exited.

As they approached his black, shiny, new BMW, he said, "This is mine," then opened the door for Rosetta. After she was seated comfortable, he closed the door, went around and got in on the driver's side, and pulled off.

"This is a nice ride you have," she said.

"Thank you," Robert responded, trying to keep his eyes on the road and off of her.

During the drive to Rosetta's house, Robert used the time to get better acquainted with his new love interest. "Tell me something about your parents," he said.

"Well, I lost my mother first and then my father a year later," she told him. "I'm an only child, so my parents left me the house and money."

Robert smiled, knowing they had the same testimony.

"Why are you smiling?" she asked.

"You may not believe this, but the same thing happened to me," he replied, then shared with her about his parents.

By this time, they were parked and sitting in front of her house.

"We sure did get here fast," Rosetta commented.

"Yes, we did," Robert agreed. "I would love to keep in touch with you. May I have your phone number?

Rosetta smiled. "Only if I can have yours."

From that point on, they started dating and fell deeply in love with each other. After seven months of dating Rosetta, Robert called Pastor O'Neil and discussed how he felt about her. He asked the pastor if he could give him space in church for him to propose to Rosetta. Pastor O'Neil said yes and asked Robert to let him know the day prior to when he planned on asking Rosetta to marry him.

One week went by, and it was a sunny, warm day in May. As usual, Robert picked up Rosetta so they could attend church together. Knowing what he had planned, he was so excited. That Sunday, Pastor O'Neil's sermon was about Love, and the theme was *I'm not ashamed to tell the world that I love you!* (Mark 8:38)

After the word came forth, Pastor O'Neil said, "I'm pausing to give Brother Robert Love some space to demonstrate this word that I have been preaching about."

As Robert stood and took the microphone, his hands began to shake uncontrollably. He was feeling God's Holy Spirit all over him. When he started speaking, tears ran down his masculine face.

"I'm not ashamed to tell the world that I love Jesus. I do love Jesus!" he shouted with conviction. "And I'm not ashamed to tell the world that I love Sister Rosetta Ann Mathis!" He paused and looked at Rosetta before continuing. "Sister Rosetta Ann Mathis, will you please come down here to the altar?"

With her mouth half open in shock, she approached the altar, and knowing what was coming next, the tears began rolling down her pretty face. Once she reached him, Robert took hold of Rosetta's left hand.

"Rosetta, I love you. It was love at first sight when I first met you in this church on that cold, but sunny October day." He kneeled down on bended knee, pulled out a small red velvet box, opened it, and after removing the ring, he slid it on the ring finger of Rosetta's left hand. "Rosetta, I love you, and I want to spend the rest of my life with you. Will you marry me?"

With tears of joy running down her face, she answered, "Yes, I will marry you, Robert Love!"

Still holding her left hand, he stood up from his kneeling position, and then they wrapped their arms around each other and gave a short kiss out of respect for being in church.

The congregation began to clap and praise God, as Robert and Rosetta thanked those who congratulated them on their engagement while they returned to their seats smiling and holding hands.

"Praise God!" Pastor O'Neil said, gaining the church members' attention. "Will there be another who will come and receive Jesus so you can come and stand with boldness as Brother Robert did. Tell the world that you are not ashamed to say that you love Jesus."

Moved by the sermon, seven men and four women came forward to receive Jesus as their personal savior.

After church service, Robert and Rosetta went to Robert's house to decide on a wedding date, as well as other things. They talked and laughed for hours, having fun planning out some of the details.

"That was fun," Robert said when they finished.

"It sure was," Rosetta agreed.

They embraced and began to kiss. Once they stopped, Robert said, "I love you so much, Rosetta," while looking deeply into her eyes.

While staring back at him with the same passion, Rosetta replied, "I love you more."

"I don't think so," he said. Then they both smiled before holding each other in another tight embrace.

"Are you hungry?" Robert asked.

"Yes. I guess I've calmed down enough to eat," she replied with a giggle.

Taking Rosetta by the hand, Robert led her to the dining room where the table was set for a romantic dinner for two. A pretty white lace tablecloth and red lace runner covered the table, and in the middle were four tall white candles and one red rose candle. The set up was so pretty and romantic.

Robert pulled the chair back for Rosetta to sit. Then he proceeded to light each of the candles. As he lit the red rose candle that was positioned in the middle of the white ones, he said, "This one represents you, Rosetta. You're as pretty as this rose. I pray this moment will always be in your heart, and that if it is in God's will, we will grow old together while our love grows with us."

"Robert, I am always full of words, but you leave me speechless. You're everything that I prayed for when I was a child. Now the time has come, and I feel as though I'm dreaming and don't want to wake up."

"Well, you're not dreaming," he told her. "God blessed us with each other, so let's enjoy each other. Now, you sit here while I serve you. You will have plenty of time to serve me, but right now, I will serve you. So, just relax and enjoy."

As Robert began putting the food on the table, Rosetta said, "You prepared all of this by yourself?

"Yes. For you, I will do anything."

Finally, all the food was on the table. They chated while chewing, and after dinner, they even had room for dessert.

"I really enjoyed this candlelight dinner," Rosetta told him. "It was great."

"I'm glad you enjoyed it."

Wanting to be helpful, she said, "Let me help you clean up. That's the least I can do."

Since it was getting late and he had to get her home, he allowed her to assist him with cleaning up.

Once they finished the dishes, Rosetta said, "It's getting late, but I'm not ready to go home after all of this excitement I've had today.

Robert smiled. “You don’t have to go home yet. How about we go in the living room and watch this good movie I recently purchased?”

“That sounds good to me,” she replied.

However, before they could get halfway into the movie, they fell asleep, with Rosetta’s head resting on Robert’s chest and his arm cuddled around her shoulder.

The next morning, Robert and Rosetta freshened up before he took her home. She had to go to work, and so did he.

After that night, they met up each evening. Sometimes Rosetta would spend the night, and sometimes she would go home, which was hard to do.

Finally, a month had passed, which seemed like a year to Robert and Rosetta. Their wedding day had arrived ––June 30th. It was a sunny, warm day. The birds were singing, and the trees seemed extra green and full of life. That day, Rosetta Ann Mathis became Rosetta Ann Love, and the newlyweds carried on with their plans.

They had decided to sell the house that Rosetta’s parents willed to her, and she moved in with her husband to enjoy their new life together. Eighteen months later, they were cuddled up in their living room on a cold night, with the fireplace blazing and the lights dimmed as they watched a movie.

“Robert, I have something special in the oven for you,” Rosetta said, pulling his attention from the television.

“Oh yeah? What is it?” he asked.

“You’ll see in seven more months.”

Confused, Robert replied, “Why do I have to wait for...” But, before he could finish his sentence, he caught on to what she was telling him and jumped up with joy. “Rose, are you telling me that you’re pregnant?”

Rosetta smiled widely. “Yes!”

With excitement, he asked, “When are we going to have our baby?”

“I told you in seven months,” she replied with a laugh. “I’m two months pregnant.”

“When will we know if it’s a boy or girl?”

“You can know right now, if you want,” she answered.

“Wait a minute. You already know the sex of the baby?”

Rosetta responded, "Yes, but before you ask me what is it, I want to know which would you prefer, a boy or girl?"

"Rose, it doesn't matter to me whether it's a boy or a girl. All I'm asking God is for our child to be healthy."

Rosetta smiled. "Okay. Brace yourself," she said, while Robert waited with excitement. "It's a baby girl that's in this oven waiting for seven more months so she can come out."

"Oh, Rose, I love you so much," he declared, hugging and kissing her. Then he rubbed her belly and said, "How are you doing in there, Ruth?" Pausing, he looked up at Rosetta. "I don't know where that came from, but if it's alright with you, let's call her Ruth."

"That sounds good to me, Robert."

Seven months went by, and on July 30th, Ruth Love was born. Robert and Rosetta enjoyed raising their little girl, Ruth Love. They called her Love. Robert followed his parents' steps with him, raising their child up in church with Godly principles. Five years passed, and Ruth Love had grown into a sweet, pretty little girl. She had her daddy's shy ways and her mother's spunk. She would always walk around the house singing along with the gospel songs that her parents had playing throughout the house.

Having seen, heard, and felt the anointing that God had given Love with her gift of singing, they decided to let her join the God's Precious Jewels Children Choir. They felt that since she was five years old, she could understand some of what she was singing, and when Love would lead a song, her powerful anointed voice would touch her father. He would flash that proud father smile, her mother would cry tears of joy, and the church would stand in praise.

Love was so gifted to sing and touch others at such a young age. She loved going to church because she had fun with her friends in the children's church, while learning the word of God, and she would go home every Sunday and explain what she had learned to her parents. What a blessing Love was to Robert and Rosetta.

Slipping in Sin

Chapter One

Mr. John Nelson and his wife Gwendolyn were Robert and Rosetta's neighbors. They had moved next door to the late Mr. and Mrs. Theodore Love forty years ago. Since they never had children, they were very fond of Robert. They had watched him grow from an infant to a twenty-four year old young man, who was now married and had a child of his own.

The Nelsons, who were in their seventies, couldn't move around as good as they did when they were younger. They were on medication due to some health conditions, and both were overweight. Dr. Donald Williams had advised them to move into an assisted living home that would provide some recreation for them. That way, they could get in a little exercise during the course of the day and live more comfortably.

After discussing it with one another, Mr. And Mrs. Nelson decided to take their doctor's advice, especially since they weren't getting any younger. The hardest thing for them was moving away from Robert, Rosetta, and five-year-old Ruth Love. However, Robert assured them that he and his family would come to visit them as often as they wanted them to and that they would keep in touch throughout the week by phone contact. So, the Nelsons put their house up for sale.

They received a lot of responses right away for the beautiful two-story house. Inside there was wall-to-wall royal blue carpet and three bathrooms, one on each floor and another in the finished basement. The kitchen had oak cabinets, a dishwasher, a washer and dryer, an electric oven, and the floor was covered with Armstrong yellow and white square tiles.

The Nelsons had no problem selling their dream home to someone who would enjoy it as they had done. The new owners were the Joneses––Leroy, his wife Mary

Christine, and their three children, Scorna, Bobby, and Billy.

While the Nelsons were getting settled in their comfortable seniors condominium, the Joneses were getting settled in their dream house.

One week had gone by since the Joneses had moved next door, and Rosetta said to her husband, "Honey, I'm going to go next door to introduce myself to our new neighbors. Do you want to go with me?"

"No," Robert replied. "You can go. I'll meet them later."

Rosetta took Ruth by her hand. "Come on, Love. Let's go and meet our new neighbors."

Love smiled and said, "I hope they have a little girl that I can play with."

After walking up the steps, Rosetta rang the doorbell and waited for someone to answer.

Mrs. Mary Christine Jones, a pretty, slender, dark-skinned lady looked through the peephole and said, "Who is it?"

"Hello. My name is Mrs. Rosetta Love, and I'm your next door neighbor. I have my daughter with me. We came over to introduce ourselves, if it's okay with you."

Mrs. Jones opened the door. "Hello my name is Mrs. Mary Christine Jones," she said, while shaking Rosetta's hand. "Please, come on in."

As Rosetta entered, she complimented on the nice natural colors that were throughout the entire downstairs.

"This is my daughter," Rosetta told Mary. "Her name is Ruth Love, but we call her Love."

Mary leaned down, smiling and looking into Love's pretty eyes. "Well, welcome to my home, Love."

Rosetta stood there with a smile on her face, trying to figure out the type of family the Jones were. She then handed a bottle of apple cider that she held in her hand over to Mary. "I brought you a little something to welcome you into our neighborhood. I hope you like it."

"Thank you," Mary said, taking the gift.

"My husband is home resting. He had a hard day at work, but he will meet you and your family at a later date. Maybe we can plan a lunch or dinner so all of us can get together."

Mary nodded her head and replied, "That would be nice. My husband didn't get home from work yet."

By this time, her three children had come in the

living room, and Mary began introducing them. “This is our daughter, Scorna, and our sons, Bobby and Billy. Children, these are our new neighbors, Mrs. Love and her daughter Ruth, who they call Love.”

Mary continued, “Children, Mrs. Love and I will plan a nice gathering so your fathers can meet each other with all of us here together. How does that sound?”

The children smiled their approval with the idea.

Scorna grabbed Love by the hand and said, “Come on, Love, I’ll show you my big dollhouse.”

The two boys went back to what they were doing, while Rosetta and Mary got aquatinted.

It seemed like only five minutes had passed, but fifteen minutes later, the ladies were still going on. While getting a tour of the kitchen, Rosetta noticed the kitchen clock.

“Oh no, time sure flies. We have to leave now so I can prepare dinner for my husband. Again, welcome to our neighborhood.”

“It was nice meeting you,” Mary said.

“If there is anything you need help with, feel free to ring our bell. We’ll talk soon,” Rosetta said as she prepared to leave.

Mary yelled for Scorna to bring Love so they could go home. Love got what she hoped for, a little girl next door she could be friends with.

Little did the Love family know that Mr. Jones had some bad issues he had never dealt with. Now with his daughter inheriting some of his issues, he didn't have a clue as to what was happening to his only daughter.

Mr. Leroy Jones Jr. was a handsome, light brown skinned, 27-year-old young man. His hair was natural black with pretty waves. He had a complex about his height since he was less than six feet tall.

His father, Leroy Sr., was so jealous that he would lie to his wife on his son. During Leroy Jr.'s childhood, Leroy Sr. would say his son did things and then send him to his bedroom in order to get all of his wife's attention.

Leroy Sr. told his wife he didn't want any more children because that would take too much of her attention. As Leroy got older, his father would send him on errands to have all of his wife's attention.

Leroy Sr. never cared about neglecting their only child and son. He wouldn't let his wife go anywhere without being there with her. This went on until Leroy Jr. turned eighteen and moved into an apartment.

Leroy met Mary Christine in an Acme market one cold December day. Mary was walking to the cash register to pay for her items, when she dropped a roll of paper towels.

Leroy bent down to hand it to her.

“Thank you,” she said.

“You’re welcome.”

They began talking about the weather and how they dreaded going back out in that cold. One topic of discussion led to another until they had reached the cash register. After paying for their groceries, they left together.

Leroy opened the door and asked Mary, “Do you have a ride?”

“Yes, my car is right there.” She pointed to her new silver Dodge Caravan.

“Let me help you with your bags then.”

She accepted his help and got in her van.

“I would like to talk to you again. Can I have your number?” Leroy asked.

“Yes.”

Mary gave Leroy her number, and from that point on, they dated, the two fell in love, and of course, they got married.

Mary never knew her parents. Her mother died giving birth to her, and her father gave her up for adoption. On the other hand, Leroy's parents lived in Maple Woodrobe Nursing Home. Each of his parents had a stroke, which left them paralyzed on one side. They shared a room at the nursing home and needed around-the-clock care. Leroy Sr. was 76-years-old, and his wife, Joyce, was 74-years-old.

One Saturday afternoon, Love and Scorna were outside playing. when Scorna said, "Love, I want to go to church with you tomorrow."

Love responded, "I'll ask my parents, and you ask your parents when we go inside to eat dinner. Okay?"

Scorna quickly replied, "No! I wanna go ask them now!"

Scorna ran and left Love standing there. So, Love went in her house to ask her parents, as well.

"Sure, Scorna can come to church with us if it's alright with her parents," Rosetta told her daughter.

Mary told Scorna that she would speak with Rosetta later in the evening when the two met on the porch.

Both parents had said yes, and the girls came back outside jumping with joy.

Laughing, Love said, “You can go!”

Scorna said, “Yes, I can go!”

Later that evening, Rosetta and Mary sat on the porch talking.

“Scorna asked me and my husband if she could go to church with Love tomorrow. We told her yes, if it was alright with you.”

“We should be leaving about 9:45 in the morning and be back home about two o’clock in the afternoon.” Rosetta said

“That’s fine with us. We will be here when you come back,” Mary told her.

The two girls continued to play while their mothers talked. Scorna was swinging a jumping rope, which accidently hit Love in the face and caused her eye to swell up immediately. Love ran on the porch.

“Mommy, Scorna hit me in the eye by mistake with the rope.”

By this time, Scorna had run up on the porch. She didn’t know Love had told her mother it was an accident.

Scorna quickly said, “I didn’t hit Love.”

Both parents responded, "It's all right, Scorna."

"We know it was a mistake. Love already told us what happened. Accidents are going to happen," Rose explained.

Mary asked, "Scorna, did you tell Love you were sorry?"

Scorna never said she was sorry. Instead, she stuck to her lie that she didn't hit Love. This was the beginning of Love witnessing the lying characteristic of Scorna. Love noticed when Scorna lied she would look down at her nose.

Mary, Rosetta, and the two girls went into Rosetta's house to put an ice pack on Love's eye, and a short while later, the swelling began to go down.

Mary said, "I'm sorry about what happened."

"That's alright. You see the swelling is going down. Things happen when children are playing," Rosetta told her.

"I have to leave now. I'll have Scorna ready to go to church with you tomorrow."

They all said good night.

As Rosetta tucked Love into bed, Love said, "Mommy, why did Scorna lie and say she didn't hit me with the rope even though it was a mistake? Scorna did hit me with the rope, Mommy."

"Sometimes when children think they are going to get in trouble, they lie. I'm not saying it's alright to lie. I'm saying some children do lie. Don't you lie, though. You keep telling the truth."

"But, Mommy, I can't understand why she still lied. She saw she wasn't going to get in trouble."

"Love, just make sure you don't lie. It's easier to tell the truth, because when you lie, you forget what lie you told. But, when you tell the truth, you can tell what happened the same way every time."

"Mommy, when Scorna lies, she looks at her nose."

Rosetta smiled, not really paying attention to what Love had said.

Love laid her head down to go to sleep. Tucked in, she began to say her prayers. She prayed, "God, I thank you for my friend Scorna. Thank you for her going to church with Mommy, Daddy, and me tomorrow. Please let us have fun. And, God, please help Scorna not to lie again. In Jesus' name I pray. Amen!"

"Amen," Rosetta chimed in. "Good night, Love."

"Good night, Mommy."

Robert was asleep already.

"Mommy, tell Daddy good night when he wakes up."

Rosetta smiled. "Alright, Love. Good night."

Early the next morning, Rosetta went into Love's room.

"Love...Love, wake up. It's time to get ready for church."

Love rolled over with joy. "Okay, Mommy. Scorna is going to church with us today. We are going to have fun in church, and she can meet some of my friends. I'm happy, Mommy."

Rose just smiled.

The Love family had taken their baths, gotten dressed, and were sitting at the breakfast table eating.

Robert spoke to Love. "I heard you had a little accident yesterday while you were playing rope."

"Yes, Daddy, but I'm okay now."

Robert looked at his wife, and they both smiled.

"Daddy, I'm happy Scorna is going to church with us today," Love said. "We're gonna have some fun. She's gonna meet my friends."

While they were eating and talking, the doorbell rang.

"I'll get it." Robert stood from the table.

When he opened the door, it was Mary and Scorna.

"Good morning," Mary said. "We're your next door neighbors. I'm Mary Christine Jones, and this is my daughter, Scorna."

"Welcome to our neighborhood." He shook her hand. "I'm Robert Love. My wife, Rose, has been telling me about you. Please, come in."

Mary and Scorna entered the Loves' home.

"Good morning, Rose. Good morning, Love," Mary said, "Did I come too early?"

"No, you're alright. We're almost finished eating. Would you two like to have some breakfast?" Rosetta asked.

"No, thank you. We've eaten already. I'm sorry to intrude on you," Mary apologized.

"You're not intruding. You're fine."

"Well, I'm going to leave Scorna with you. I will see you when you get back from church." Mary then looked at her daughter and said, "Scorna, you be good, or we won't let you go to church again with Love. Do you hear me?"

"Yes, Mom, I hear you. I'm going to be good."

Love watched Scorna look down at her nose as she told her mother the lie.

"Good. I will see you all later."

Everyone said goodbye, and then Rosetta turned the TV on for Scorna to watch cartoons. Once the Loves finished eating breakfast, they got their jackets, and Robert drove them all to church.

The girls went downstairs to the children's Sunday school, while Robert and Rosetta went to morning service in the sanctuary.

As Love, Scorna, and the other children were enjoying their Sunday school lesson, Scorna asked Love about the bathroom. Wanting to show Scorna where the bathroom was located, Love raised her hand to ask for the teacher's permission.

Love waited as Scorna went to the bathroom, and after the girls washed their hands, they returned to the room. When the teacher noticed water running from the bathroom to the classroom she ran into the bathroom, saw a roll of tissue in the toilet, and realized somebody had to just put it in there.

Knowing Love and Scorna were the last two inside, she called them to the bathroom and asked, “Who just used that toilet?”

“Scorna did,” Love answered.

“No, I didn’t. Love did,” Scorna said, while looking down at her nose.

The teacher sent Love and Scorna up to Robert and Rosetta with a note telling what had happened. The Loves came down from their service to ask what happened. Robert told the girls if they didn’t tell the truth, they couldn’t come to church together anymore.

Scorna, while looking down at her nose, said, “I was trying to take tissue off the roll, and it fell in the toilet.”

From then on, the girls would come to church, but they had to stay upstairs with Robert and Rosetta. Love didn’t care as long as Scorna could come with her. Eventually, Scorna stopped coming because she couldn’t get into trouble while sitting upstairs under the Loves’ watchful eyes.

Three months went by. It was September and time for the girls to start kindergarten.

Love and Scorna went to the same elementary school one block up the street from their homes. Although they were in different classes, they would see each other during recess.

One day as they played, three girls came over to them and asked, “Do y’all want to play rope with us?”

“Yeah, I want to play,” Love said.

“No! I don’t want to play,” Scorna yelled.

“I’ll take an end and turn,” Love offered, joining the other girls.

Scorna snatched the rope out the hand of one of the girls. “I’ll turn, too.”

The girls played with a single rope. As the first girl began to jump, Scorna deliberately yanked and turned wrong. The girl tripped, fell, and skinned both of her knees. She started crying, and one of the teachers took her to the nurse’s office.

“Why did you do that, Love?” Scorna demanded.

“I didn’t turn the rope wrong. You did. You made her fall and hurt herself.”

Scorna looked down at her nose. “No, I didn’t! I didn’t want to play this old, stupid rope anyway!”

Scorna changed the subject as though nothing had happened. “Come on, Love, let’s go play hopscotch.”

Scorna quickly grabbed Love's hand, and they both ran to the hopscotch game. A few games went by before the bell rang.

Scorna kept doing evil things against Love and others. She continued to lie and say she wasn't responsible. Love was the only one who noticed how Scorna looked down at her nose when she lied.

While Love always forgave Scorna, others wouldn't play with her, would call her a liar, and thought she was trouble. This went on through elementary, junior high, and high school.

Twelve years had gone by, and the girls were seventeen. Love and Scorna were in the twelfth grade and were searching for colleges to attend. Love decided she wouldn't tell Scorna which college she was going to attend because Love didn't want to put up with Scorna's evil, lying spirit any longer.

Scorna kept asking Love which college she picked, but Love wouldn't tell her until Scorna told Love which college she had picked and was accepted in. When Scorna didn't look down at her nose, Love knew Scorna was telling the truth.

"Now will you tell me which college you're going to?"

Love finally gave in. "I was accepted at Mount Pleasant College. So, that's where I'm going."

The girls talked a little while longer, and then Scorna left.

Scorna couldn't wait to get home and start making phone calls to Mount Pleasant College. There was a spot open since one person changed their mind at the last minute. So, Scorna was accepted in Mount Pleasant College, as well. Scorna didn't tell Love, though. Instead, she wanted to surprise her.

Summer came and was gone. The girls were to report to Mount Pleasant on Monday, August 14th. The first day, Love settled in her room. As she walked down the hall, Scorna walked up behind Love and covered her eyes.

"Surprise! Guess who?"

Love turned around fast in shock, recognizing Scorna's voice.

"Scorna, what are you doing here? I thought you were going to St. Luke College?"

Scorna looked down at her nose. "It was a mix up with me and this other girl's name. Her name was Scorna, too. Once I heard there was an opening at this college, I decided to come here."

Love smiled. “Oh. Well, where’s your room?”

“Two rooms down from yours,” Scorna said, pointing to her door.

As the two girls kept walking and talking, one of Love’s friends that they went to school with came up to them.

“Hey, Love.” She looked at Scorna, knowing she was a lying troublemaker who had a jealous spirit. “Hey, Scorna,” the girl said dryly and then kept walking by.

Love’s roommate was Cindy, a white, pretty, slim young lady with long, straight, blonde hair. She was also easy to get along with.

Cindy walked up. “Hi, Love!”

“Hi, Cindy!” Love said, before turning to introduce Cindy to Scorna.

When different people who went to school with Love and Scorna saw Scorna, they whispered to each other about her evil spirit.

“Why is Scorna here? She’s a liar and a troublemaker. We heard she was going to St. Luke’s.” They asked each other what happened, but no one had an answer. None of the young ladies wanted Scorna in college with them, but as before, there was nothing they could do about it.

Three months went by, and Scorna and Love were getting along fine. Scorna was staying out of trouble, but began to get confused and frustrated. She couldn't catch on to the schoolwork or keep up with the teachers.

After seeing Cindy leave, Scorna runs over to Love's room and asks Love does she have any sugar she can borrow.

"Sure. Wait a minute," Love said, then got the sugar to give to Scorna.

"How are you doing with your term paper?" Scorna asked.

"I did fine," Love replied. "I'm finished, and I think I did well. All I have to do is turn it in to Mr. Greg."

"I don't know why I'm having a problem with mine. This college thing is not working out too good for me," Scorna expressed. "Can I see your term paper? Maybe I can get an idea from yours. I'm glad we're in the same class."

Scorna watched as Love went to retrieve her term paper, which she kept under her bed in a briefcase.

Once Love showed Scorna her term paper, Scorna said, “That’s good, Love. Thanks for letting me see your term paper. Now I have an idea of what Mr. Greg wants.”

Later that night, Scorna visited Love again. They were the only two in the room. After they talked for a little while, Love excused herself to go to the bathroom. That’s when Scorna went under Love’s bed and took her term paper, which had to be turned in the next day. What Scorna didn’t know is that Love had an extra copy in the same suitcase, but in an inside pocket.

As soon as Love returned from the bathroom, Scorna said, “It’s getting late. I think I’ll go work on my term paper.”

“Okay, I’ll see you tomorrow in class,” Love told her. “I hope you get it together.”

While looking down at her nose, Scorna replied, “I’m halfway finished, so I’ll be done tonight. I got a good idea from yours.”

Then they both said good night.

The next day in class, the girls turned in their term papers. Confused, Scorna looked on as Love turned hers in. Love didn’t know her first term paper was missing, because when she went in her briefcase, she reached in the inner pocket without thinking and pulled out one of her two copies, while Scorna had the original one she had stolen.

A week went by before the professor, Mr. Greg, called Love and Scorna into the dean's office. Mr. Cameraman, who was the dean, Mr. Greg, Love, and Scorna were present while Scorna had the original one she had stolen.

"We have a problem here," Mr. Greg stated.

"What's the problem, Mr. Greg?" both girls asked in unison.

"I received the same term paper from both of you, the exact same wording. Can either of you explain this to me and Mr. Cameraman?"

Love looked over at Scorna as she looked down at her nose and said, "I don't know what happened, Mr. Greg. I did mine."

"May we see them, Mr. Greg?" Love asked.

"Sure, this is yours, Love, and this is yours, Scorna."

"Mr. Greg, if I may be excused?" Love said. "I have a copy in my room. I made three copies in case something happened."

"Yes, go and get your copy," he told her. While Love was gone, Mr. Greg asked Scorna, "Do you have another copy of your term paper?"

Scorna replied, "No."

When Love returned to the dean's office with her copy, she said, "Scorna, I can't believe you would stoop this low. One of my copies is missing. You had to take it when I went to the bathroom last night after I showed you where I kept it. How could you do this to me? What if I didn't have extra copies?" Love then looked at Mr. Greg and said, "This is my work. I have no reason to lie."

"Scorna, what do you have to say?" Mr. Greg asked.

Mr. Greg and Mr. Cameraman had already agreed if Scorna admitted to stealing Love's term paper, they wouldn't search her room. However, if she admitted to doing it, they would give her a written probation and have Scorna apologize to Love, Mr. Greg, and Mr. Cameraman.

With her head hanging down, Scorna said, "I'm sorry, Love. I'm sorry, Mr. Greg. I'm sorry, Mr. Cameraman. Yes, I stole Love's term paper. This work is getting too hard for me, but I don't want to dropout of college."

Scorna then looked down at her nose and added, "I didn't want to get Love in any trouble."

Mr. Greg and Mr. Cameraman stuck to their plan of disciplinary action by giving Scorna a written probation letter. They both expressed they were sorry about what happened to Love, and before dismissing the girls, they told them not to mention it to anyone.

The two girls walked out of the dean's office quietly, and once outside, Scorna said, "Love, I know you won't trust me again, but please let me still be your friend. I don't have any friends in this place. I don't know what I'll do by myself."

"Scorna, I just can't figure you out," Love responded. "I keep trying to hang in there with you, but you keep doing things behind my back. I could've gotten into big trouble."

Looking down at her nose, Scorna said, "I promise not to do anything else to or against you."

"I'm going to pray on this, Scorna. I will talk to you tomorrow."

"Okay, Love. I'll see you tomorrow."

That night, Love talked to God, saying, "God, I'm tired of turning the other cheek when it comes to Scorna.

She's been doing me wrong for a long time now. I try not to come to the same college with her, but even with that, she tricked me and winded up in here with me anyway. I thank you, God, for protecting me each time she does things against me. I could have gotten into big trouble, but you let me know that you got my back. God, please continue to help me by watching my back. I don't know what Scorna is going to do next, but I'm going to hang in there with her a little longer, God!"

Even though Love didn't mention the incident to anyone, someone had seen Love and Scorna when they went into the dean's office, and they eavesdropped. Having heard the whole conversation, that person spread the word about what had happened.

"Why does Love keep letting Scorna hang with her when she knows Scorna doesn't mean her any good?" Love's friends would say.

When word got back to Scorna that everybody knew what she had done to Love, Scorna stopped speaking to Love, thinking she was the one who had put the word out.

If that's how she feels and doesn't want to speak to me, that's fine, Love said to herself. *I don't have to watch my back anymore. I can't trust her anyway.*

One month later, Scorna went to Love and said, "I remember when we were best friends and had good times together. Let's make up and be friends again."

"You're the one who stopped speaking to me after you had done me wrong," Love reminded her.

"I know, but I thought we came to an agreement that we weren't going to tell anyone about what happened. Why did you tell?"

"I kept my agreement," Love told her. "I don't know who spread the word about what happened. I did hear that some guy had eavesdropped that night we were in the dean's office. I guess he heard everything and began telling it all over campus."

"It's okay. Let's put it all in behind us. Can we be friends again?" Scorna asked.

"Yes, but only if you will stop lying. It doesn't make sense the way you keep lying the way you do!"

"Okay. I'll try to stop," Scorna said, while looking down at her nose, "but how do you know when I'm lying?"

"It doesn't matter. You're going to stop lying, and that's all that matters," Love replied.

Three weeks went by, and everything was going fine, until one day when Mr. Greg had the test on his desk that he was going to give to the class in a few days.

Mr. Greg held the test up in front of the class and said, "I have the test ready that I'm going to give you. This one is going to be a little easier than the last one. So, study, and be ready to take your test next week. Now, you may be excused."

Scorna pretended like she was still copying the lesson from the board. Everyone had left except her.

Mr. Greg's cell phone rang. Since he had bad reception inside the classroom, he stepped out into the hall for not even a minute, leaving his briefcase open. Scorna rushed up to his desk and took the test paper from off the top of Mr. Greg's suitcase. Then she ran and sat back down.

When Mr. Greg walked back into the classroom, Scorna got up and said, "See you next week, Mr. Greg."

"I'll see you next week, Scorna," he told her before closing his briefcase and rushing out the room.

Before the start of class the day of the test, Mr. Greg prepared for his lesson, and that's when he noticed the test paper was missing.

"Now I know I left the test paper in this briefcase so I wouldn't forget it."

He kept looking, thinking, and tracing back where could it be. Then he thought back to that day when he had left Scorna in the classroom for a minute while he went in the hallway to take a phone call.

That's right! She was copying the lesson from the board, he thought. *I don't believe this girl. I remember her having a similar situation with Ruth Love's term paper. Well, she's in big trouble now.*

He went and talked to Mr. Cameraman, and they decided that was it for Scorna. She had to leave Mt. Pleasant College.

In the meantime, the day of the test, Love and Scorna were sitting in Love's room talking, when Love's cell phone rang.

"I can't hear you. Wait a minute," Love said, then stepped outside of her room for a minute.

Scorna started quickly looking around the room. She had studied Love's surroundings for so long that she knew what books Love carried and where they were located.

Scorna looked over at the dresser and said to herself, "There goes her books." She then slipped Mr. Greg's test paper in Love's books and quickly sat back down on the bed.

"I have to go, Scorna," Love said when she came back in the room. "I will see you in class in a few."

"Okay, see you in class."

Two hours had passed, and it was time for the students to assemble together in class. Mr. Greg let everyone get seated and settled down. The students were ready to take the test they had studied for.

Mr. Greg stood up and started pacing back and forth in front of his desk, while looking at the whole class, especially Scorna. He was going to wait until class was over before he talked to Scorna.

"I'm sorry," Mr. Greg told his students, "but I have to cancel your test until next week because someone stole the test paper I had ready for you to take today."

He looked at Scorna, who held her head down the entire time he was talking.

“If anyone knows or hears anything, let me know,” he continued. “And if you think of anyone who would have the nerve to come up to my desk, go into my briefcase, and steal the test I had prepared for you, please let me know.”

Knowing what Scorna had done to Love three weeks prior, the entire class, including Love, looked over at Scorna.

“Open your books to page seven,” Mr. Greg said, ready to start the day’s lesson.

When Love opened her book, Mr. Greg’s test paper fell out of her book and drifted to the floor.

Love picked it up, looked at it, and said, “Wait a minute!”

She spoke so loudly it caught everyone’s attention, including Mr. Greg’s.

❦Chapter Two❧

"Mr. Greg, is this the test paper you're looking for?" Love asked. "I just opened my book, and it fell out on to the floor. I didn't do it."

By this time, Love was walking the paper up to Mr. Greg while crying and thinking, *Scorna did it to me again. How am I going get out of this one?*

Mr. Greg told Love to stop crying and that he thought he knew how it got there. Love wiped her eyes with relief and returned to her desk as she looked at Scorna, who was sitting with her head hanging down, looking at the floor.

When Mr. Greg saw there was so much tension in class, he told the class, “Be prepared to take the test next week. You’re dismissed.” Then he said, “Love and Scorna, I want to see you two. Stay in your seats please.”

The whole class whispered amongst themselves as they were leaving the classroom, saying, “Scorna did it. She needs to be kicked out of this college. She keeps trying to get Love in trouble.” They all walked out, spreading the word about what happened.

After everyone had left the room, Mr. Greg called the two girls up to his desk and asked, “Scorna, do you have something to say to me?”

“No,” Scorna replied while looking down at her nose. “I don’t know what you’re talking about.”

Love started crying and blurted out, “Yes, you do. You’re lying again. How could you keep trying to get me in trouble like this? It’s time for you to tell the truth and stop lying. You got caught again, and I’m tired of your mess!”

Frustrated and tired of Scorna’s mess, Love stood with her right hand balled up in a fist ready to punch Scorna.

"I should knock you upside your head. Maybe you will get some sense and stop doing the evil things that you do to hurt people!"

Mr. Greg stepped between the two girls and said, "Love, two wrongs don't make a right. Scorna is already in trouble. You don't have to get in trouble with her. It's not worth it. You are doing fine in Mount Pleasant College. Let me and Mr. Cammerman settle this matter."

Taking her professor's advice, Love calmed down and backed away from Scorna.

"Scorna, a few weeks ago, we went through a similar experience when you stole Love's term paper," he said. "You have to first admit that you did this, and then we can deal with it."

"I didn't want us to have to take the test," Scorna confessed. "I'm sorry!"

"But why would you put the test in Love's book? Didn't you know she would get blamed for it?"

Now it was Scorna who started to cry. "I don't know why I do these things to Love. I like Love. I don't understand it."

For a change, Scorna wasn't looking at her nose. She was actually telling the truth.

"I have already taken this to Mr. Cammerman. I was going to call you up after class because I traced back to when I noticed the test was gone. I remembered that last night in class when everyone left but you. I had left you in the classroom for a minute to take a call, and that was the only time you had to take my test paper. Am I right?" Mr. Greg asked.

"Yes, but I'm sorry, Mr. Greg. I'm sorry, Love. I'll apologize to the dean. Just please don't kick me out of college."

Mr. Greg responded, "It wouldn't be fair to Love or the rest of the school if we keep on tolerating this from you. It's not fair that Love is trying to make it through college, but can't concentrate because you keep doing things against her and putting pressure on her like this."

He paused for a second to let his words sink into Scorna's head. "You can't keep going on like this. The class was ready to take their test, and they couldn't because of what you did." Mr. Greg directed his attention to Love. "I'm sorry you had to go through this. You may be excused."

Mr. Greg then said to Scorna, "Come on. We're going to Mr. Cammerman."

That day, Scorna was dismissed from Mount Pleasant College.

After four years of college, Ruth Love returned home, moving back in with her parents. Her parents no longer attended church because they were both sick and taking medicine.

One week later, Love got a job as an assistant to the administrator of Newton Hospital. She was doing fine and preparing to start her new job. One day, who did she run into but Scorna, who was coming out of her house while Love was going into hers. They greeted each other with a hug.

"I didn't know you were home," Scorna said. "Did you finish your term in college, or are you just home for a visit?"

"I finally finished college," Love told her. "I got my Bachelors Degree in medical technology."

They stood for a while exchanging words and sharing with each other how life had been since they parted ways.

"I have two sons, but they live with their father," Scorna told her. "We just got a divorce," she added, while looking down at her nose. "He wasn't faithful to me, and I couldn't take being married to him anymore. So, I came back here to live with my mom and dad."

"How is everybody else?" Love asked.

"Mom and Dad are doing fine. Bobby still thinks he's a lover and God's only gift to women. Billy has two sons who both live with their mother. Bobby and Billy still live here at home, as well. How about you, Love?" she inquired. "I see your parents all the time. Moving slow but getting around good."

Love said, "Yeah, Daddy has arthritis in his right side. He has some good days, while other days he can barely get up from sitting or laying. Mom has hypertension. Despite them both having health issues, I thank God they are still here and have each other for support. They don't go to church anymore due to Daddy's condition. I keep Daddy and Mommy in my prayers daily. I will start working at Newton Hospital tomorrow. God has blessed me with an assistant position to the administrator there." Love then pointed to her car and said, "Look at what else God has blessed me with."

While looking down at her nose, Scorna replied, "I'm happy for you."

"I'll be talking to you," Love said, cutting the conversation short.

"My number is the same. Call me later, or can I call you."

"I'll call you later," Love told her before walking away.

Later that night, Love called Scorna just as she said she would.

"Hi, Scorna! I'm not going to stay on the phone long," Love informed her. "I'm getting my clothes ready for work for tomorrow. In case we don't see each other no more this week, I'm calling to ask if you want to go to church with me this Sunday?"

With joy, Scorna replied, "Yes, I'll go to church with you. What time do you want me to be ready?"

"I'll be leaving about 10:45 in the morning. I'm driving, so it won't take us but a few minutes to get there," Love said before ending the call.

Both girls didn't see or talk to each other for the rest of the week. When Sunday came around, just like old times, they were excited to go to church.

Pastor O'Neil preached a good sermon. The theme was "It's Time to Work for God." After the sermon came altar call. Love and Scorna walked down to the altar to renew their faith. By being so busy while in college, they had stopped going to church. Scorna had stopped attending to church long before they went off to college, though. Love stopped after she had gotten in college. It felt good to come back in fellowship with God again.

Two months later, Love had joined the choir and usher board. Of course, Scorna joined the same two boards. Things were going fine, until the sisters started paying more attention to Love because of her peaceful and nice spirit. Love had a gift of greeting people with a smile, and she would always encourage any and everyone with God's word.

Scorna's jealousy started rising up again. Love joined the hospitality board, and Scorna joined the following week. Love was voted to be the president of the hospitality board. The board had planned to give a free calendar luncheon. They had twelve tables with the twelve months of the year. Their plan was to set the tables to match what occasion usually occurred during that month. For example, November's table would be decorated with a centerpiece in the middle and setup to resemble a Thanksgiving Day dinner. Everyone on the board had agreed what foods and decorations to bring.

Scorna went around and told a few sisters that Love said they didn't have to bring vegetables because there were plenty, but for them to bring more meat. Trusting Scorna's word, the sisters didn't bother to confirm the request with Love.

When the day of the luncheon arrived, there was plenty of everything except for vegetables.

"I don't know what happened," Love said. "Oh God, what do I do now? Okay, Lord, I'll go and get some canned string beans. They don't have to cook long."

Everything turned out fine. There was more than enough vegetables, and everything was successful.

A week after the calendar luncheon, Love called a meeting so the board could come together and discuss how well the calendar luncheon went along with a few other things. Love expressed to the members that everything turned out fine. She told them that they had more than enough food and that they tripled the money they had put out to have the luncheon.

Love said, "God willing, we will plan to go to the Sight and Sound Theatre to see Behold the Lamb of God, if we are all in agreement of doing it. How does that sound?"

Everyone said it sounded good to them, except Scorna, who didn't say anything.

"Good," Love replied. "We can do this, but we have to be on one accord!" Love then asked the sisters, "What happened to the vegetables for the luncheon? We were short on vegetables in the beginning of the luncheon, so I went and bought some canned string beans. That's why we had more than enough at the end of the luncheon. Some of you that were assigned to bring the vegetables didn't bring them. What happened? We have to be in unity or else God won't bless us, and if God doesn't bless us, the people will miss their blessings. We will be at fault because we are messing up others' blessings."

Confused, one of the sisters who Scorna had relayed the false message to spoke up. "Sister Love, at first, you told us to bring vegetables, and then you sent Scorna to tell us to bring meat instead because you had enough sisters bringing vegetables."

Love looked at Scorna, who habitually looked down at her nose.

"I didn't say that," Scorna lied. "I told them that you said to bring meat and a little vegetables."

The sisters that Scorna had told the lie to looked at each other and said, "That's not what you told us, Scorna."

Love knew Scorna was lying, so to stop the confusion, she told them, "Okay, next time if a situation comes up like that, if I don't come to you myself, stick with what we agreed upon. I'm glad everything turned out fine despite the mess up."

After the meeting was over, while everybody went their separate ways, Scorna approached one of the hospitality board members and said, "Love don't know what she's doing. She needs somebody to call everyone up and check to see if everyone is on one accord the night before our functions. I told her that I would do it, but she told me that she didn't need anyone's help!"

Soon, word began to spread that Love don't want anyone to assist her because she wanted to run the board by herself and just have the others do what she told them to do.

No one confronted Love, but they would talk to each other about it. The sisters on the board became very rebellious and started doing things against their president. Love noticed it, but she didn't know Scorna was stirring trouble up. Having heard of the strife on the hospitality board, Pastor O'Neil called a meeting.

"The board has to sit down until they can learn to get along and love each other," he told them. "I'm doing all this preaching in the church about being aware of the devil and his tricks. Yet, you all let your guard down for him to come and cause much confusion."

Scorna looked at Love and smiled deviously.

Scorna had stirred up so much trouble, but nobody on the board saw what she had done to Love. One minute, they had voted Love to be the president of the hospitality board, and the next minute, they pulled her down. Love felt so alone. Pastor O'Neil never bothered to ask Love what was happening. He had just heard the rumors going around.

Six months went by, and Love decided she would work for God in another zealotry by joining a choir. She had joined another choir at the same time she joined the hospitality board, but as soon as Scorna joined, Love left the choir. Scorna also left not longer after Love.

"Even if Scorna joins this choir, I'm not going to leave," Love told herself. "Lord, I will sing for you just as I did when I was younger. Please help me to stand strong and not let Scorna run me off from this choir."

Scorna didn't join, though. Instead, she became the president of the hospitality board that Love had been forced to step down from. Scorna continued to stir up so much trouble on the board that they were getting ready to be sat down again. All the while, Love was enjoying singing for God. Souls were being healed, delivered, saved, and set free from bondage.

One year went by, and Love was still enjoying singing on the jubilee choir. When the time came to install new officers, Love was nominated to become the choir's president. Upon hearing this, Scorna soon joined the choir.

The choir was doing fine, until one day at a choir meeting, Love said, "It's been a year that we've been singing. It would be nice if we had a fundraiser to raise money for the purchase of some choir robes. What do you all think?"

Everyone was in agreement but Scorna.

"Robes are too hot during the summer months," Scorna expressed.

Everyone looked at her as if to say, *Don't come on this choir starting your mess.*

Some of the sisters on the choir had heard about the mess Scorna stirred up against Love on the hospitality board. They also knew their choir never had any problems prior to Scorna joining, and they were determined unity was going to stay amongst the members of this choir.

It was voted that they would have a fundraiser to get choir robes, and they reached their goal. Dressed in their new robes, the choir sang under the anointing of God, and the church continued to receive blessings time after time.

Again, Scorna began stirring up trouble. It was a hot summer day, and everyone came in the choir room with their robes. Love had put hers on the clothes rack and left the room for no longer than a minute. When she returned, her robe wasn't where she had hung it.

"Did anyone see my robe?" Love asked. "I hung it here to go to the bathroom, and when I came out, it wasn't here."

Scorna said, "Can we not wear our robes today? It's too hot for these robes anyway."

While looking at Scorna, Love asked in front of everyone, "Scorna, did you see my robe?"

"No, I didn't see your robe," Scorna replied, while looking down at her nose.

Oh my God, Love thought to herself, *Scorna is starting her lying again. She knows where my robe is.*

"I have a suggestion," Love said. "You all go ahead and sing. I'll sit this one out. You all can sing a few songs we rehearsed that you don't need a lead person to lead."

Everyone shook their heads at her request.

"No, Love, we rehearsed with you, and we're going to sing with you," one of the choir members voiced. "If it's alright with you, we will still wear our robes. You won't look out of place since you're the leader of the songs we're going to sing."

"Alright," Love replied, giving in.

After they formed a circle holding hands, one sister ended the prayer with, "Lord, please help Love to find her robe."

They said amen together and then went out into the sanctuary. God moved the choir like never before, and everyone in church got blessed.

At the end of service, the choir returned to the choir room, and before anyone could take their robe off, Love said, “Look, there goes my robe.”

She then looked at Scorna, remembering Scorna had gotten up to go to the bathroom in the middle of the service. Everyone in the room was so quiet that if a pin dropped, you would have heard it. After a few moments of silence, the choir members started to remove their robes in preparation to leave the church. A few mumbled amongst themselves, being curious to know how Love's robe had been put back without any of them knowing who had taken it.

Once Love and a few of the sisters went to the bathroom, Scorna said to the other sisters remaining in the room, “Wasn't that strange how Love's robe suddenly showed up after we sweated our butts off in this heat singing with these robes on? I think Love left her robe in the bathroom this morning when she went to the bathroom.”

Another sister responded, “You know, Scorna, you may be right. Love did go to the bathroom.”

Instead of them saying Love could have forgotten her robe in the bathroom, they begin gossiping. A few sisters walked away, while a few sisters stayed to hear Scorna talk about Love.

When Love came back from the bathroom, she heard the tail end of the conversation. “I didn’t leave my robe in the bathroom,” she said, defending herself. “I checked in the bathroom I was in, and it wasn’t there.”

The sisters who were with Scorna walked out the room whispering about Love, saying, “Love lied. She didn’t want to wear her robe because it was too hot, but we had to wear ours.”

From that point on, Scorna had herself a little gossiping clique. Scorna felt if she could get Love removed from the choir, she could run for president of the choir. Little did she know, everyone on the choir wasn’t blind to Scorna’s evil ways. Some of these sisters were praying for Love and the whole situation, because they had picked up on Scorna’s jealous, evil spirit. Scorna went around the church spreading rumors about

Love. Eventually, the word got back to Pastor O'Neil so he called a meeting with the choir.

"I don't know what's going on with this choir, but I do know we can't sing for God while at the same time keeping mess going on," he told them. "You are setting a bad example for the church with all of this bickering."

"Pastor O'Neil you don't have to sit the choir down as you did with the hospitality board when I was on it," Love said. "I will sit myself down. It seems like I keep being a problem in this church."

"Love, if that's what you want, I will be praying for you," Pastor O'Neil responded.

Love looked at Scorna, and Scorna smiled. The sisters that were praying about the situation never spoke up. Love walked away with her head hung down, as if she didn't have a friend in the world. After going into the bathroom where there was no one, Love began to talk to God.

"God, you see everything that's going on. Yet, you say nothing or do nothing. Scorna put these rumors out about my parents and me. She says I have been frustrated with Mommy and Daddy, but, God, you know I don't argue with them. You know that I've been depressed about what's going on in this church, but Mommy and Daddy keep telling me to pray on it. God, you said you would fight my battles and that all I have to do is stand. Well, God, I've been standing, and I am tired of standing by myself."

By the time Love walked outside to get in her car, she had made up her mind that she wouldn't be returning to church anymore.

Love went into a deep depression. She would go into her bedroom, staying away from her parents. The only time she came out of her room was to eat, take a bath, or go to work. When she went to work, she stayed to herself and had no conversation with anyone.

One hot, sunny day in June, Love was in her bedroom having a pity party. She got in her bed and covered her whole body, including her head, with a king-size quilted blanket. Love felt as though no one would ever understand what Scorna had been doing to her for the longest.

Love had a conversation with God, but God didn't say a word back to her. This caused Love to feel neglected and rejected by God. So, she became very angry and turned away from God.

"God, it seems like I have to do wrong before people notice how I was trying to live a holy life the best I knew how serving you," she said. "God, everywhere I turned I felt a thorn in my side...from the church, not the world. I know I could have taken the thorns better if they had come from worldly folks. At least I would understand that they don't know any better because they are not serving you, God!

"I'm tired of it, God. You said you would put no more on us than we can bear. Well, God, I can't take no more of this so-called church of yours. The weight from the church is too heavy for me to bear. I have been through the fiery furnace time after time. I have been on trial by the church. I have been misused and abused by the church. My kindness has been taken for weakness by the church. The church has misunderstood me. My name has been scandalized by the church about things I didn't do. God, I have been through sickness of depression because of the church. I have been hurt so bad.

"God, I feel so alone. I feel like I'm the only one that love has forgotten. You are supposed to be love; the church is supposed to be love. I have been crying myself to sleep for a long time now. I'm tired of going to sleep and waking up to the same hurt. God, I...quit...you! I need a God that is going to hear me and answer me back when I talk to him."

Chapter Three

The very moment Satan heard Love complaining and telling God that she wanted a God that would hear and answer her, Satan started talking to Love, and she began to talk back to him.

Satan told her, "Get up. You don't have to feel like this. Go buy yourself something nice, low-cut, and skimpy--something that will catch any guy's eye. Then get ready and go down the street to the bar. It's two-for-one night. When you go there, a young man will be sitting at the bar. The church has hurt him, too. He will be waiting to hear from you.

Love used to get excited when God would give her instructions. Now she was excited about the instructions Satan was giving her. Love felt happy and relieved not to be experiencing any more pain from being hurt by the church.

That night, she got dressed and was on her way out the door, when her mother asked, “Love, where are you going dressed like that?”

“Mommy! Daddy! I’ll be all right now! I quit God! I quit the church! I’m tired of talking to a God that sees and knows my hurt and pain, but won’t talk back to me. I need a God that will hear me and answer my prayers Mommy and Daddy, you use to go to church, but you stopped going when you got sick. I thought you had the faith that God would heal you! But, you can’t tell me anything because you quit God first. So, don’t try to talk me out of doing this.

I quit God, just like you quit God. Don’t worry about me. I’ll be fine now. I don’t have any more pressure on me from that church. I won’t stay out too late. This is the best I have felt in a long time,” she expressed, then began walking away.

Mr. Love was speechless. He had never experienced his daughter in the state she was in, going out dressed in skimpy attire. She was not the precious daughter that he and his wife had raised.

“Honey, stop her,” Mr. Love said to his wife. “Talk to her. We can’t let her go out dressed like that.”

“Let her go, honey,” Mrs. Love replied. “I don’t want to fight with her. My blood pressure is already up. If she thinks she’s old enough to make a decision like this, let her go. We will stay here and pray her, though, because she’s going to need it. We raised her the best we could. She will come to her senses one way or another. We have to put her in God’s hands and leave her there. God will take care of her. Honey, I don’t have the strength God does, and He will take care of our daughter. He gave her to us temporarily, but she belongs to God forever. We’re going to have to trust God. We have to let go and let God handle Love, while we do what loving parents should, which is stay here and intercede for our one and only daughter. She’s going to need prayer as she falls so that we can help her back up. Trust me, honey, Love will be all right one way or another.”

Robert and Rosetta embraced in a hug.

"I thank you, honey, for letting God use you to say the right words," Robert told his loving wife. "We will be here for our daughter, and I know God will take care of her. I'm happy you didn't let Love run your blood pressure up more than it is already. I need you, Rose. I can't imagine what I would do without you. We have to take care of each other. Let's draw strength from each other and let God take care of Love. We have raised her the best we could. Now we are going to put her in God's hands and leave her there."

They walk upstairs to their bedroom and turned the television on to watch a movie. But, exhausted, they both ended up falling asleep with the television watching them. On the flip side, Love was on her way to slipping into sin.

*****

When Love arrived at the bar, a young man was already there sitting on a bar stool. His name was Sonny, and he was a tall, brown-skinned young man.

"Wait a minute," Love said. "I've seen you in church before. What are you doing here?"

"I was about to ask you the same question," Sonny replied. "You used to sing on the choir. I used to love to hear you sing. It would bless my heart. So tell me what happened."

"I quit the choir, I quit the church, and I quit God! I got tired of all the drama in church. My neighbor Scorna kept stirring up bad rumors about me, and the church kept judging me. Every zealotry I got on, the pastor would sit it down instead of getting to the bottom of what was really going on." By this time, Love had taken a few sips of Bacardi Lime. "I thought pastors heard from God. I wonder why God didn't tell him what was really going on!"

The young man responded, "They are supposed to hear from God, but I don't know why they don't hear from God when they are saints!"

"Because they are not saints! Running the good folks out of the church. You'd think God would show the pastor exactly who's the troublemaker," Love voiced, then asked, "What happened to you in church that made you leave? Why did you quit God?"

"I didn't have a position in church, and those with positions kept looking down on me and wouldn't let me utilize the gift that God has given me," Sonny told her. "I didn't want a position or a title. I play the organ. I just wanted them to let me know what I had to do in order to use my gift of being a skilled organist. They treated me like I came to church to take their gift, title, or position!

"I guess God took my gift back since I quit him, as you would say. It was no use in having a gift that people don't let you use anyway," he said. "You know, church can be very boring if you're just a member sitting there hearing the word of God from the pastor. God said to use the gift he gave you, but they won't let you use it. I just don't understand that!

Sonny then changed the subject. "That's enough talk about the church. Let's talk about you. I wanna know more about you."

At that moment, a song came on, and the crowd started line dancing.

"Do you know how to do the line dance?" Sonny asked.

Love replied, "No, but I'm willing to learn."

"Come on, let's go," he said, taking Love by the hand and leading her to the dance floor.

Love caught on as if she had been line dancing for years. When that song went off, a slow song came on next.

"There's no use in us sitting back down now," Sonny told her. "Come on, let's slow dance."

"I know you're not gonna believe this, but I have never slow danced before either."

"That's all right. You can learn this, too," Sonny responded as he took hold of Love's right hand. "Put your hand up like this, as if you were giving me high-five." He then locked their hands together and put his left arm gently around Love's waist. "Now all you have to do is rock slow with a little groove in it while I lead you."

As she swayed with him, he said, "Yeah, you got it." Whispering in her ear, he asked, "What's your name?"

She whispered back in his ear, "My name is Love."

"I love that name," he replied in a hushed voice.

Continuing to whisper in his ear, Love asked, "What is your name?"

"My name is Sonny."

By this time, Love noticed Bobby there with a young lady; they were slow dancing, also. Bobby was Scorna's oldest brother. He was a player. He didn't have one girlfriend; he had a string of girlfriends. The girls had Bobby thinking he was God's only gift to women. Bobby stared at Love, frowning upon seeing her. Knowing that Love had always been active in the church, he was puzzled as to why she was in the bar slow dancing with some guy he had never seen before. Love looked at Bobby with some guilt at knowing she used to be a saint but had lost her way.

When the song ended, everyone who had been dancing returned to their seats.

Bobby came over by himself and asked, "Hey, Love, what are you doing in a place like this? I belong here, but you don't. You're a good girl."

"I'm doing fine, Bobby," Love assured him. "Don't start talking that goody stuff to me. I'm not trying to hear that right now."

"Well, will you at least introduce me to your friend?" he said.

"Sonny, this is Bobby, my next door neighbor. Bobby, this is my friend Sonny."

After the two guys shook hands, Bobby said, "Let me go back over to my honey. See you later."

Bobby couldn't wait to get home to tell Scorna about Love and Sonny.

After Bobby walked away, Love told Sonny, "I'm ready to leave now."

"Can I take you home?" Sonny asked.

"Thank you, but I'm driving."

"Well, can I walk you to your car?" he offered.

"Sure," Love replied.

Once at her car, Sonny opened the door for her to get in it. "I had a good time with you."

Love says, "I enjoyed myself, too," she responded, then looked back at the bar to see Bobby peeping out the window looking at them.

"Can I have your phone number?" Sonny asked.

After the two exchanged numbers, Sonny closed the door of the car and watched as Love drove off. He then went to get in his car.

All the while, Bobby watched out the window of the bar so he could see what kind of car Sonny was driving.

Man, I wish she were my girl. I can get any girl I want, but Love has never even looked at me in that way, Bobby thought to himself while watching Sonny pull off in his car.

*****

The next morning, Bobby walked to Scorna's room and knocked on the door. "Scorna, are you awake?"

"Yeah, what do you want?" she called out.

"Can I come in?" he asked.

After Scorna granted Bobby access, he said, "Guess who I saw in the bar last night with some guy named Sonny?"

"Who?"

"Love!" Bobby told her.

Scorna shouted, "Who?"

"Yes, Love! I was shocked, too. Sis, she looked so good. What happened to her and church?"

Scorna looked down at her nose and said, "She couldn't get along with a few sisters in church, so she left."

"Yeah, right! Love gets along with everybody. She was getting along with Sonny last night," Bobby said, laughing. "You were probably the reason she left church.You were always jealous of Love," he added while walking out.

Scorna smiled and threw her teddy bear at him. "Get out of here!"

Scorna couldn't wait for Bobby to leave her room. She rushed to dial the phone number of one of the church sisters.

"Girl, guess who my brother said he saw in the bar last night?"

The sister on the other end of the phone said, "Who?"

"Miss Holier Than Thou--Love!"

"What?" the sister said in disbelief.

Immediately upon ending their conversation, they called around to all of the other gossiping sisters that were in the Scorna's clique.

*****

The day after Love went to the bar, her phone rang. It was one of the deacons from church, trying to show Love the church's concern about her.

"Hello," Love answered.

"Praise the lord. This is Deacon Carr. May I speak to Sister Ruth Love?"

"This is Ruth Love," she replied.

"Sister Love, I noticed that you haven't been in church for a few weeks now. Is everything alright?"

"Yes, everything is fine with me, Deacon Carr," she told him. "I quit the church, and I quit God.

"Love, the church is here to help you. I'm sorry you feel the way you do," he said. "You have many gifts that folks need. Your ministry is not finished in this church. We need you."

"Thank you, Deacon Carr, but when I was in the church, nobody seemed to care about me. My name was being misused and abused by your church. I have been on trial by your church, and your church has misunderstood me. I'm tired from the weight of the phony people in your church. You have sisters in your church that are always talking about me and waiting to tear me down. If that's what church is about, I don't want no parts of church anymore!"

Love continued, "I talked to God all the time about what was going on in your church, but God wouldn't answer me. I feel as though God is judging me."

"Sister Love, listen to what you are saying. God is not answering you, so he must be judging you? Well, you are judging God! Just because God doesn't answer us when we want him to answer us, doesn't mean God is judging us," Deacon Carr told her, then shared a testimony about himself. "One time, I asked God an important question, and I didn't hear the answer until one year later, but when God answered it, I needed the answer right then. God is an on-time God. He answers when he's ready."

"Deacon Carr, you're one of the nicest deacons in that church. I expect a good word coming from you because you always encourage people in the church. But, please tell the church not to call me anymore because I have quit the church."

Deacon Carr responded by saying, "I respect your request, and I will relay your message to the church. But, Sister Love, you can't stop us from praying for you."

Love simply replied, "Okay, Deacon Carr," and then they both said goodbye.

From that day on, Love started going to different bars and clubs with Sonny every week. One day, Love went to a club that she and Sonny had gone to before. Sonny wasn't expecting her nor was she expecting to see Sonny. However, when Love walked in, she saw Sonny and Scorna all hugged up and kissing.

Walking over to a waiter who was standing nearby, Love picked up a drink from off of the waiter's serving tray and then walked over to the table where Sonny and Scorna were sitting.

"You two deserve each other!" she yelled while pouring the drink on both of them.

Unable to say anything, Scorna just sat there with a shocked look and her mouth wide open as Love walked away.

Sonny ran after her, saying, "Wait a minute, Love." Love kept walking, though. When she got outside of the club, she cried while running to her car.

By the time Sonny got outside, Love was gone. So, Sonny walked back in the club and said, "Come on, Scorna. Let's go.

*****

Love began falling deeper into sin. She went out by herself throughout the week and on the weekends, meeting different guys who did nothing but use her body. Then she wouldn't see them anymore. Bobby would see her from time to time, but she wouldn't speak to him because she couldn't stand Scorna and didn't want to associate herself with anyone or anything that had to do with Scorna.

One night, Love went to an after-hour spot that everybody went to if they wanted to hang out some more after the clubs and bars closed. That's where Love met Slick Rick, and he was slick just like his name. He knew how to slick talk any woman into what he wanted from them.

Love was sitting at a table by herself, when Slick Rick walked over and asked, "Can I sit here?"

"Yes," she replied.

"What's your name?" he asked her.

"My name is Love. What's yours?"

"My name is Slick Rick."

"Oh boy, here we go again," Love said. "You're one of the slick guys who thinks he can get over on every woman, aren't you?"

"No! I got my name from how I dress," Slick Rick replied. "Look at me. Do I look slick or what?"

He was so slick; he took Love's thought off his name and put it on his clothes. He used this same line on all the women, and they would fall for it. As they would look at his clothes and how fine he was, they would start to give in to Slick Rick. He had Love's mind blown, too.

"Love, may I buy you a drink?"

"Sure. I can trust you, can't I?" Love answered.

He went to get their drinks, but before he came back, he put a drug in Love's drink.

When he returned to the table, he said, "Look," and then pretended to drink some of Love's drink. He touched the top of her glass with his lips so fast that it appeared to Love that he had actually taken a sip.

"I know you can't trust anybody these days," Slick Rick told her, and Love fell for that, too.

Not long after Love finished her drink, she said, "Woo! It's time for me to leave. I'm feeling a little tired and have had enough to drink for the night. Will you please walk me to my car?" she asked Slick Rick.

"I sure will."

Slick Rick walked Love to her car, and after looking all around to make sure no one was watching, he pushed her inside and raped her, leaving her laying on the backseat all drugged up.

A few hours went by, and Love began to wake up. All she remembered was Slick Rick walking her to her car and pushing her inside. She vaguely recalled him being on top of her as she tried to fight back while screaming for him to stop. Then she passed out. When she woke up, she had no clothes on and felt soreness between her legs from being raped.

Suddenly, Love heard the voice of God say, "Love, hurry! Put your clothes on fast. Slick Rick is coming back with three more guys. They plan to rape and kill you this time."

Since the drugs hadn't worn off completely, Love tried to move as fast as she could and finally made it to the front of her car. Half-dressed, because she couldn't move fast enough to put on all of her clothes, she sat in the driver's seat with only her slip and bra on. She was moving in what seemed like slow motion. Just then, she noticed a car pull up and park.

Scared, Love began to call on Jesus. "Please help me, Jesus! I need your help. If you help me, I'll come back to you. Please don't let me die here like this. Please help me, Jesus!"

Every time she attempted to put the keys in the ignition, they would fall on the floor of her car because her hands were too shaky.

"Jesus, why won't you help me!" she screamed. "Please forgive me and help me. I need you. Satan set me up!"

By this time, all four guys had gotten out of their car and were coming towards Love's vehicle. She knew it had to be God that put the key in the ignition, because she couldn't do it no matter how hard she tried.

She heard one of the four guys saying, "Hurry up! She's getting away!"

He grabbed the door handle of Love's car, and Love dragged him to the ground as she pulled off, until he let go. Then, Love picked up speed, and by the grace of God, she made it home safely. After pulling up in front of her house, she picked up her dress that was on the passenger seat and slipped it on. She didn't know where her shoes were, so she got out of her car barefoot and in shock about what she had just gone through. Still scared, she kept looking around. She couldn't get in the house fast enough. Finally, she put the key in her door and was inside safe. By this time, she was more alert.

As she walked up the steps slowly, Mrs. Love came out of her room and asked, "Love, are you alright?"

"Yes, Mommy, I'm alright. I just need to take a shower and be alone."

When Mrs. Love went back in her room, she said to Mr. Love, "I guess she's alright. She's moving slow, but she says that she's alright. I know God hears our prayers, and Love is not going to go on too much longer like this!"

Inside her room, Love removed the clothes she had on and threw them into her trashcan. She then wrapped a towel around her, went into the bathroom, and turned on the shower. After stepping inside the shower, she crouched in the corner of the shower with her elbows resting on her knees and her hands holding her head that was lowered. As the water ran over her body, she began talking to God.

"God, I know it was you that spoke to me, and I know you started the car for me because my hands weren't steady enough to put the keys in the ignition."

By now, Love was more alert and aware of what had just happened. God flashed everything back to Love as she sat in a daze under the shower with tears running down her face. God showed her from the time she went in the club where she met Sonny the first time up to now while she was sitting in the shower.

Chapter Four

"Love, trials come your way to build you up, not tear you down," God called out to Love and said. "You've read and heard my word about Job, time after time, in many different ways, with the same meaning. Job lost everything he had in order to gain it back with more. Those storms came Job's way to demonstrate to the body of Christ that I may not come when you want me to come, but I am an on-time God. I come when I'm ready to come according to the purpose. I've seen and know everything you have endured. Who do you think brought you from every trial you went through?

"I don't ask any of my servants do they want to go through what they have to go through. If I did, they all would say no! If I asked *you* to go through what you went through, *you* would have said no! You had to experience all you went through in order to go and help others who are going through some of the things you have been through.

"Love, folks do just what you did to me. First, most of them come to me after being hurt by the devil, and then after I heal them and get them back on their feet, they quit me and go back to the devil.

"In your case, I allowed your parents to raise you up in the church. I allowed the devil to come to you because I have chosen you to go through, to build you up so you can stand anything that comes your way. I built you up so you will have faith that I will help you no matter what comes your way, and you will know this without a doubt.

"Love, I heard you when you said you quit me, but even though you quit me, I didn't quit you! I have been covering you ever since you quit me. I said in my word that I will never leave you nor forsake you. I will never leave you or quit you, or my word would be a lie in the book of John 14:18, according to what I inspired John to write. Just like the words of "Footprints in the Sand" that were written, when you were at your weakest moments, I was carrying you.

"Love, you lost your esteem in me. You gave up and quit me. As this was suppose to happen to show the believers what happens when they think they can make it without my help.

"I'm calling you to another level in the ministry, Love. Some folks are waiting to be ministered to, and I have given you the goods. Folks are about to quit me, just as you did, but I'm not going to let them quit me. I'm ready to use you to go and tell them your testimony. They will hear me through you. They will get delivered, and then I will use them, too. Love, you can't have a testimony unless you have been through a test. You have been in the fiery furnace, and I was in there with you. I helped you out, and you have no traces of being burnt. I have given you a glow that will draw my people to me.

"Love, I will call you my evangelist. Man will try to call you something else, but just pray for them and continue to do what I instruct you to do. Some folks have the title of an evangelist, but you have the gifts of the evangelist and will do the work of such.

"Now, get up! Go back to church! Your brothers and sisters are hurting, and they need me. I'm ready to give them ME through you! Many are called to do this task; many are chosen to do this task. I have called and chosen you to do this task, in the book according to Matthew 9:37. I left my word as a reminder to my disciples as well as my servants today, knowing that the harvest will always be plentiful but the laborers will always be few. Love, get up and go do what you must do!"

Love asked God, "But why did you let Slick Rick rape me? You could have stopped him, God!"

"Love, stop focusing on the rape. I didn't let Slick Rick kill you. Just like I told Satan in the book of Job, 'Whatever you do to Job don't touch his soul. His soul belongs to me.' So I was with you no matter what happened. Slick Rick couldn't kill you because your soul belongs to me.

"Sometimes you, as well as my people, put yourself in predicaments that I have to get you out of, and that's what I did. I didn't let Slick Rick and the other three guys rape you again and then kill you. If I did, everything I've been telling would be in vain."

God continued, "Love, stop blaming me and others. Get yourself back up, and as you do get up, all the hurt will be gone and you will have a new beginning. Don't worry about Slick Rick. You will hear soon how Slick Rick has gotten killed by a young lady, whom he drugged and raped a few days ago."

Love stood up in the shower. "God, please forgive me for quitting you. Please help me to focus on you and do everything you want me to do and that is pleasing to you."

She then started washing, while smiling and saying, "Thank you, Lord. I can smile again. I feel the presence of your spirit again. Tears of joy ran down her face, mixing with the shower water. "God, forgive me for judging you; forgive me for quitting you; forgive me for not having faith in you; and forgive me for treating my body the way I did."

Love continued to praise God. "Thank you, God, for saving me from Slick Rick and the other three guys that were coming back to rape me. I thank you, God, for warning me of them coming back. Thank you, God, for washing me in this shower with this water of the world, as well as with your spiritual water. God, please continue to be with me."

*****

Sunday came, and Love walked into the church while the choir was singing, "I won't turn back. I won't turn back. My heart is fixed. My mind's made up. No, no, I won't turn back."

When Deacon Carr saw Love walk in, he began praising God, saying, "Thank you, Jesus! Thank you, Jesus! Hallelujah! Hallelujah! Hallelujah!" Tears fell down his face as he continued to praise God."

As Love approached the altar, the choir stopped singing in order to hear what Love was about to say.

"I know why Deacon Carr is praising God so hard," Love began. "Because he never stopped praying for me, and this is the result of his prayers. I have learned from God through Deacon Carr that God will answer our prayers when he wants to—to whoever he wants to—how he wants to—and wherever he wants to. I learned that he's an on-time God whenever he answers our prayers."

Love continued, "Praise God. I'm back, and I'm coming back stronger than before. Like the choir was singing when I walked in, I won't turn back. My heart is fixed. My mind is made up, and no, I won't turn back! God picked me up and turned me around. He placed my feet on solid ground again. He sent me back to this church that I was brought up in. Please forgive me for being so weak and for quitting you and my God the way I did. If you help me, I will assist this church the best I know how with God leading me."

The whole church stood up and started clapping.

Pastor O'Neil stood up and clapped, as well, while saying, "Welcome back, Sister Love!"

Deacon Carr went over to welcome Love with a big hug and a smile. "Praise the Lord," he said. "Welcome back, Sister Love. I will be working with you. Don't let no one run you away from God again!"

By this time, the choir had started singing the same song they were singing when Love walked in.

As the Spirit of God began to calm everyone down, Pastor O'Neil began preaching the sermon for the hour. His sermon came from the book of Matthew 8:24-27. The topic was

If You Hold On, Jesus Will Calm Your Storm. After the word, Pastor gave the invitation to Christ, and two sisters received Christ as their personal savior. He prayed for them, collected the offerings, and dismissed the church.

Saturday of that week came, and Love was in the living room relaxing while watching the news on TV. Slick Rick's picture flashed up on the screen. Love's eyes spread open with shock. The reporter was saying that a young man, Rick Benson, known as Slick Rick, had been killed by a woman whom he raped and drugged a few days ago. The woman voluntarily turned herself in and would be awaiting trial. She wanted her name kept anonymous.

Love had wondered if she was going to run into Slick Rick in the future. God took the wonder from her mind, though. She was relieved that she didn't have to wonder about it anymore. Love had made up in her mind when she had gotten rape that she wasn't going to tell no one about her rape assault, that it was between her and God. She felt as though she would have been treated as the victim, so why bother?

A few weeks go by, and one Sunday morning, guess who walked in church? Scorna! She walked in the church and sat down next to one of her girlfriends. They greeted each other with a hug and a kiss. Pastor had preached a sermon titled *When God Touches You, You Won't Be the Same*. After he finished preaching, he opened the altar for a call to discipleship and for those who wanted to rededicate their life back to Christ.

"Will there be one that will come and let Jesus touch you?" Pastor Lionel asked the congregation.

As Scorna began walking down the aisle, she repented out loud, saying, "I'm sorry, Jesus!" By time she reached the front of the altar, tears were running down her face as she shouted, "Jesus, please forgive me for all the wrong I have done to everybody! Please forgive me for everything I've done wrong to Love! Jesus, please touch me. I need a touch from you. If you touch me, I know I'll be able to live right, love right, and treat everybody right!"

While she spoke, Scorna did not look down at her nose. Scorna was being honest! Love looked at Scorna, with the tears running down her face as she was repenting, and Love knew she was for real this time.

Love's feet got light, and she began running up and down the aisles of the church while shouting, "Thank You, Jesus!" She couldn't keep still; the Holy Spirit was controlling her. Finally, she fell down face first to the floor, but luckily, she didn't hurt herself. One of the ushers covered her with a Lapp scarf as she lay on the church floor. That's when God began to speak to her.

"Love, I could trust you over this one soul, Scorna. I know she put you through a lot, but you didn't give up on her. There were times when people didn't understand why you wouldn't let her go, why you kept forgiving her each time she would do evil things to you. But, you passed the test. Some people have to retake this test because they can't stand the pressure of being misused and abused. I have anointed you to pass this test, and even though you called yourself quitting me, you never let the love of me go! That love will always be in you. It comes with salvation. Now that you are back in fellowship with me, I will send many souls to you that I will draw to me.

"Some souls will be hateful. They have been hated for so long by the world because of their hateful ways, but I am going to draw them to me through you. Some will come to you with a jealous spirit like Scorna once had. They want what others have, and they will do anything to get it, just like Scorna did. But, it was good that she wanted what you had, because she received the salvation she wanted from you. Some women are going to come to you with hurting hearts, but I'm going to mend their broken pieces back together again through you! Some have been raped by Slick Rick. I'm going to heal them through you. Scorna will assist you, but this time, she will help you and not hinder you. Her testimony will draw souls to me, as well.

"I will establish a large women fellowship in this church. Women will come to get healed, delivered, and set free from the bondage they have been in for a long time. The atmosphere will be set so that the women will feel free to open up and talk about their problems, not feeling that it will be repeated."

That moment, God began lifting Love up on her feet. Tears were still running down her face. It seemed like she had been down on the floor for about an hour, but it was only five minutes.

God said, "I will bring everything back to your remembrance as I instruct you what to do."

By this time, the whole church, which had been in an uproar, began to settle down. Those that were slain in the spirit were just getting up. Some of the women had their wigs on crooked. One of the sisters had her ponytail in her hand, one sister couldn't find her big rimmed hat, and another sister couldn't find one of her black leather high heals, but it was all good. The Holy Spirit had come and had its way in Fishers Of God Baptist Church that morning!

With a renewed faith in God, Scorna ran over to Love and hugged her. "I am sorry for all that I have put you through," she expressed to Love.

Tears were running down both of their faces as they locked up in a holy hug and kissed each other with a holy kiss, while giving thanks to Jesus.

"Love, will you teach me how to help you in the ministry?" Scorna asked. "Just tell me what to do, and I'll do it."

Love looked at Scorna to see if she was looking at her nose, but Scorna would never look at her nose again because she was lying. God had delivered Scorna from lying as well as all of her bad ways. Still, Scorna was not going to be perfect. She would still have some issues in her life, just like everybody does. Nobody is perfect but God!

Love was so use to searching for signs that Scorna was lying that now Love had to be delivered from looking at her in that way. God would deliver Love from that, too.

"I will teach you how to help me," Love told her. "Scorna, while I was slain in the spirit, God spoke to me about you and I working together in a women fellowship that will take place here at our church in the future. I will talk to Pastor O'Neil about this at a later date."

Love continued, "I will pray to God, and I'm sure God will instruct me on what, when, where, and how to do it, and instruct me in teaching you to assist me."

After church, Love and Scorna went home with joy, telling their families what had happened. As Bobby listened, he couldn't believe what he was hearing. His sister sounded excited and different. Tears rolled down her face as she confessed about how long she had been jealous of Love. All the time, she wanted what Love had, and she had finally received it--the Holy Spirit.

"I got it. I feel it," Scorna told them as they listened intently. "I can't stop crying. He controls my tears; He controls my heart; He controls my mind; He controls my body; He controls my soul; He controls my tongue. I don't lie any more. I don't have that jealous spirit I had towards Love and others. I don't have those evil spirits in me that make me do wrong when I want to do right!

"Mom! Dad! Bobby! Billy! I feel good. I've never felt this way in my life before. You all can have what I have! All you have to do is ask Jesus to come into your life by faith, and tell him that you're sorry for living in sin. Ask Him to guide your life, and he will do it. Listen to me. You hear that I've been changed. That's the only way I'm going to see you in heaven, if you receive Jesus as God in your life!"

"You mean God will change my life, too?" Bobby asked Scorna.

"Yes, Bobby. If God can change me, he can change anyone."

He then asked, "Can he do it here in our living room, or do we have to wait until next Sunday and go to church?"

"Are you ready to receive Jesus right here, right now?" Scorna asked them.

They all responded, "Yeah!"

"Repeat these words after me," she told them, and they did as they were told. "Jesus, come into my heart. Lead and guide me. Forgive me of my sins. I do believe you are real. I believe that you died and God raised you from the dead on the third day. I do believe that your holy spirit lives on, leading and guiding people. Please give me the joy that Love and Scorna have."

Scorna then began praying for her family. With tears running down her face, she said, "God, I come to you in Jesus' name, thanking you for saving my family and my soul. Please continue to lead and guide us. Please help us to come to church as a family and learn more about you. I thank you, God. In Jesus' name, I pray. Amen!"

When Scorna opened her eyes, her mother grabbed and hugged her. With tears running down her face, she told her only daughter, "I'm so proud of you."

"I want you all to come to church with me Sunday. Will you come?" Scorna asked, praying they would agree to go, and they did.

"I don't have nothing to wear but my partying clothes," Bobby said. "Will they be alright to wear?"

Scorna told him, "God says to come just as you are. God doesn't look at a man or woman's outer appearance.

God looks at the heart of the man or woman. That's what counts with God."

*****

That night, Love called Scorna, and Scorna shared with Love what had happened. Love dropped the phone, and all Scorna could hear was Love repeatedly shouting, "Thank you, Jesus! Hallelujah!"

While Love was praising God, Scorna just listened while crying in a quiet praise.

Finally, Love picked the phone back up and said, "Scorna, I'm not going to apologize for praising God, for he is worthy of all praises."

Scorna finished telling Love that not only did her family get saved in their living room, but they were coming to church with her on Sunday.

"Praise God!" Love shouted. "See, Scorna, all that we both went through was suppose to happen for such a time as this. So that you and your family could get save."

"Yeah, Love, you went through a lot of stuff while dealing with me. I want to thank you for not giving up on me when others turned their backs on me. Regardless of the wrong things I did, you were always there forgiving me."

Love told her, "God doesn't give up on us, and we're not suppose to give up on each other. Even at our worst time, it was God's spirit that helped me to hang in there with you. I couldn't hang in there on my own. Girl, I have some testimonies about how God brought me through those times."

Love and Scorna talked for a good while before finally hanging up.

*****

Sunday came, and Love and her family came to church. Scorna and her family came to church, as well. When the doors of the church were opened for people to join, Scorna walked down the aisle with her family. Once at the front of the altar, Bobby dropped to his knees and began to cry. He didn't know why he couldn't stop crying. Deacon Carr along with a few other deacons went over to comfort him.

As they bent down next to Bobby, they told him, "It's alright. God is just touching you with his spirit. You're feeling the hand of God on you."

God then spoke to Love. "Go down and stand beside Bobby. Stretch your hands out and pray for him while the deacons are ministering to him. This man is going to be your husband."

While Bobby was getting up from his knees, with tears running down his face and his eyes still closed, he heard God's voice say, "The woman that hugs you when you get up is the woman I have chosen for you to marry. She's going to be your wife. She already knows because I told her."

When Bobby opened his eyes, Love went to him and hugged him.

"You are going to be my wife," Bobby whispered in her ear.

Love responded, "I know, because God told me that you're going to be my husband."

Nobody knew what the two were saying but them and God. As some sisters were wondering why Love was even up there with Bobby, God spoke in their ears and said, "Mind your business." They turned around to see if it was somebody else who had spoken to them. God said again, “Mind your business." From that point on, there was no more gossiping. God nipped it in the bud right then and there.

Bobby and his family joined the church and came every Sunday.

Mr. and Mrs. Love returned to church. Although their health problems hadn’t gone away, they were strong enough to come and sit through the entire service when they couldn’t before.

Love and Bobby began dating and enjoying each other. They fell in love, and just as God had said, they got married. They moved away not too far from their parents, and not long after they were married, Love got pregnant.

They were blessed with a baby girl, and Bobby insisted that they name her Scorna after his only sister who he loved so much. Wanting to please her husband, Love agreed to name their baby Scorna.

Two years went by, and Love noticed something about their daughter. Cookies were on a tray in the dining room, and when Lil’ Scorna asked her mommy if she could have one, Love told her not until after she had eaten lunch.

Love then sat her daughter at the table and went in the kitchen to get her lunch. When Love came back, Lil' Scorna's mouth had chocolate smeared all over it.

"Scorna, I told you that you couldn't have a cookie until after you had eaten your lunch. Why did you eat one anyway?" Love asked her.

Lil' Scorna looked Love right in her eyes and replied, "Mommy, I didn't eat a cookie." Then she looked down at her nose and said, "I didn't."

Love looked up towards the heavens and said, "Oh my God, please don't let this trait that Lil' Scorna seems to have inherited from her aunt continue to stay with our daughter. I see it, God, and you know it, God. Please don't let this happen to me again through our daughter."

The End

Encouragement

Some of us have been through some of the things that Ruth Love went through. I, too, was hurt while attempting to do God's work. That's how I can relate to Ruth Love's story. Everybody has a testimony, and nobody can tell it like you can. This book is to encourage: My readers to stand and don't let no one move you from where God put you! Read 1-Peter 5:8: Be sober, be vigilant, because your adversary the devil, as a roaring lion, walketh about seeking whom he may devour. To be sober means to discipline yourself and know that you can't do nothing without God. Make sure your life is all about God! John 10:10 reminds us the devil is a thief who comes to steal, kill, and to destroy every gift and everything that God has given to us.

He is waiting for the moment to set you and I up as he did Ruth Love in this story. He doesn't care who he use. A saint, family member, neighbor, co-worker, those closest to you, your husband or your wife, your children, etc. The key is to keep our focus on God. His Holy Spirit will help us to resist the devil, and he has to flee. James 4:7 teaches us this.

Don't think you are in this thing alone. Don't think you are the only one that has been hurt so bad, whether it was in church or outside of church. God comes through this story to let you know that he is omniscience (all-knowing), omnipotence (all-powerful), and omnipresence (everywhere but not in everything). When I got hurt by the church, God didn't let me leave him. He led me to another church. Unfortunately, God doesn't allow everyone to take the same route. Some folks go through hurt and God allows them to leave him, knowing he will help them back. We get hurt by our neighbors, but we don't move because of it! We get hurt on our jobs, but we don't quit our job because of it! We get hurt by our family members, but even if we disown then, they are still our relatives. No matter what we feel or say, we're still related.

Readers, no matter what we go through in life, we can't do anything without God through Jesus Christ. In John 14:6, Jesus said to his disciples, "I am the way, the truth, and the life. No man cometh unto the Father but by me."

No matter what we go through, remember that God is an on-time God. He may not come or answer us when we think he should, but when he comes through, he's on time. Some folks learn of God and then leave God. Some are so stubborn that they don't hear God, or they hear God but ignore him calling them back until they get too far out in sin and die in that state they are in.

To all my readers, if you would like to receive Jesus to have him lead and guide your life, do what the characters in this book did. Read Romans 10:9-13. Mean what you read and say. You will began to feel and experience a new beginning in your life. May God continue to bless you, and may you share your blessings with others.

Where is the Church?

INTRODUCTION PAGE

There are many stories told. Some are fiction and some are fact. God has blessed me to write both. A story is what you make it. Every story that God has blessed me to share, I have experienced and lived some part of it, which makes it easy for me to write about it. Not only have I lived some of the story, but others have experienced some of the story, as well. While reading the story, the writing will touch them, and they will realize either they have been through this or know somebody else who has been through it. In this book, I write words of encouragement to let the world know that no matter what you go through, you are not in this thing alone. Somebody somewhere is going through the exact same thing you are going through.

My testimony or somebody else's testimony will bless you as they tell you how they made it through their trials and tribulations. I can write and tell you there is a blessing on the other side. If you can stand the pulling, God will pull you through. Just hold on and don't let go!

God blessed me to write *Where is the Church?* because it's true that the saints are here to help whomsoever will come and receive the help. But, when the church goes through a crisis, the same people the church helped can't wait to tear you down with others that don't know you! My prayers are that people will read this story and realize there is a judge who sits high above and looks down on all of the judges who are wrongfully judging his people. Matthew 7:1-6 states that how we judge others we will be judge in the same way.

When I began writing this book, a sister walked up to me and said, "I heard that you write books." When I told her, "Yes, I do," she asked me the name of my next book. I informed her that my next book is a Christian novelette titled *Slipping In Sin/Where is the Church?*. The sister got so excited when I said the title, *Where Is The Church?* She said, "Yeah, that's right. Where is the church?" I stopped her and said, "Wait a minute. The book is not like it sounds. I am not writing to tear the church down. The church has been torn down for long enough. I am writing to build the church up." I then told her the church helps people, but then when the church goes through a crisis, some people are ready to tear them down. The sister shortened the conversation and walked away.

My prayers are that we will be quick to help one another and not quick to judge one another.

Chapter One

Saul L. Williams was a young man who had finished high school and went in the Armed Force. He served in the Army for four years. After his four years, he came home and began working as a supervisor for the Camden Post Office.

He was a young man that feared God and went to church when he could. While in the Army, he couldn't get to church like he wanted to do, but nothing could stop him from praying and fellowshipping with God. He had no children, nor did he have a girlfriend or wife. His parents, Wilber Williams and Flossie Williams, raised him up in church. They were the proud parents of the 22-year-old gentleman.

One hot, sunny Saturday afternoon on August 22, 1992, Saul heard the voice of God say to him, "Saul, there is work for you to do. The work is hard, and the laborers are few. I want to know if I can depend on you."

We know that God knows the answer before he asks the question to any of us. God knows where we are in ministry and life, but he wants *us* to know where we are in ministry and life.

Saul answered with joy, thinking it was a privilege and an honor for God to even consider him and call him to do work for him! He humbly considered himself not worthy. He knew he could do nothing without Christ who strengthened him, as John 15:5 teaches us. Yet, he knew he had Christ in his life, so he could do all things, as Philippians 4:13 teaches us.

He began answering God, saying, "Yes, Lord, I'll go where you want me to go. I'll do what you want me to do. I'll say what you want me to say. I'll pray what you want me to pray. Here I am, Lord. If you can use anything, Lord, let it be me that you use. I'll be a nobody telling everybody about somebody who can and will save anybody! I'll go through the storm, through the sickness, through the rain and the pain! The road may get rough at times, but I'll go. Times may get tough, but I'll go! Through all the persecution, trials, and tribulations, yes, Lord, I'll go!"

Saul was a man after Gods' heart. He was willing to be obedient to what God wanted. Although he knew he was not a perfect man, God, who was going to help him, was a perfect God.

God responded to Saul's answering to his call. "Saul, don't focus on prophecies that come your way if it doesn't line up with what I tell you to do. I am the one who has called you to be used by me to do work! I will instruct you as to which bible institutes to go to!" God then finished giving Saul instructions.

Seven years went by, and during those seven years, Saul had been doing bible schooling led by God, while also attending his home church.

God spoke to him and said, "Saul, the season is now for you to begin to establish one of seven churches."

Saul's pastor of his church, Pastor John, came to Saul and said, "Brother Saul, God has spoken to me. He said the season is now for you to begin one of seven churches. God told me to ordain you as a pastor. You have been working in this church faithfully, assisting me and this church."

Saul remembered what God had said to him. *Don't focus on prophecies that come your way if it doesn't line up with what I tell you to do.*

Smiling, Saul replied, "Praise God, Pastor, I'm ready."

A few months later, Pastor John ordained Brother Saul to Pastor Saul. Things began to happen so fast. A week after ordination, God spoke to Pastor Saul.

God said, "Pastor Saul, there is a vacant building on 11th Street. By your faith, go there and inquire that you would like to purchase it. I have a brother there looking at the For Sale sign, thinking to himself, 'I sure will be glad when somebody comes to buy this building'."

Saul went to do what God had told him to do. As he approached 11th Street, he saw a brother standing there as though he was in a daze.

Saul walked up to him and said, "Do you know how I can get in touch with the person who is selling this building?"

The brother standing there replied, "You're talking to him. I was just standing here thinking to myself that I will be glad when somebody comes and buys this building."

God gave Pastor Saul favor through this brother. The first church Pastor Saul was to establish was on its way.

Two years went by, and God spoke to Pastor Saul. "You will receive a piece of paper with a seal on it. I am elevating you to another level in the ministry! To much is given much is required." (Luke 12:48)

Pastor Saul received a call that night. It was Pastor John on the other end of the phone, saying, "Pastor Saul, God has given me another revelation concerning you. God told me to give you a piece of paper with a seal on it. He also told me that he was elevating you to another level in the ministry and that he is going to give you another level of anointing. After learning of this, I couldn't think of nothing else but having a service and letting one of the bishops come and ordain you as a bishop. Let me know what is the best time for me to make this happen for you. Then I will schedule you to be ordained as a bishop."

Two months went by, and Pastor Saul was ordained as Bishop Saul.

Bishop Saul was a Bishop, with all of the qualifications that Paul told Timothy, a Bishop should have in 1-Timothy 3:1-7

Bishop Saul was blameless. He didn't have un-Godly things that the devil, through people, could jingle over his head while threatening to expose him if Saul didn't do what he told him to do. He was a God-fearing, Holy-living man of God. He didn't have a wife yet. He was a sober man of God.

He was of good behavior and knew how to treat people.

He was self-controlled, with the help of the Holy Spirit!

He was ready to welcome strangers in his home.

He was well qualified and able to teach.

He was not a drunkard.

He was not a violent man.

He was gentle and peaceful.

He didn't love money so much that it would cause him to lose his focus from God and the people, to become a filthy lucre and rob them of their money.

Bishop Saul was able to manage his own house, and if he had children, he was the type of man that would make his children obey and respect him.

Bishop Saul did realize that if a man didn't know how to manage his own family, then how could he take care of the church? He was well mature in the faith so he would not swell up with pride and be condemned as the devil had been. Last but not least, Bishop Saul was a man who was respected and held a good report by the people in and outside of the church! He was aware that he would not be disgraced and fall into the devil's traps as long as he focused on God and maintained the qualifications of a bishop!

Every two years that went by, God would speak to Bishop Saul to go ahead and establish another church. Finally, after thirteen years, Bishop Saul established all seven churches due to being obedient, following God's instructions, and with God's favor and blessings!

Bishop Saul's mission for the seven churches was completed. Souls were being saved and added to each of the seven churches. The flow of the Holy Spirit was moving in each of the seven churches. The seven churches weren't perfect; they had some clauses in them, but God was helping them, as they would mess up from time to time.

Fast as Satan would come in the church, that's how fast he would leave out the church, because he knew he couldn't stay where God's Holy Spirit resided!

ꕤChapter Twoꕤ

The last church Bishop Saul had established was in trouble. The Neighborhood Church Of God was located on Fifth Avenue. Like all of the other churches that Bishop Saul had established, it started out with just a few members. It grew to be a church family of three hundred people and was still growing, until one day a crisis came to invade the church.

Bishop Saul had ordained and placed in this church Pastor Craig Martin, who God was using in a mighty way and doing a great work through him. Pastor Martin was married to Olivia and they had one child named Nahari. They had lived in the area for ten years and were well known in the neighborhood way before they became Pastor and First Lady of The Neighborhood Church Of God.

This particular Sunday morning during church service, the saints were having a testimony session going on. Some parents were popping up one by one and testifying about how there was a loan shark in the neighborhood named Trigger, but by the grace of God, he passed by the children that attended The Neighborhood Church Of God.

Smiley and Kevin were sitting in church this Sunday. Smiley was a eighteen-year-old man who had finished high school, but he didn't want to go to college. He was a young man with a job, just trying to make it with an honest living and live a good life. He had received Jesus as his personal Savior, and he went to church at least three times a month. Whenever you saw Smiley, he would always be smiling. That's why his mother nicknamed him Smiley.

When you saw Smiley, you would see Kevin. They were best friends. Kevin was an eighteen-year-old man, too. He lived around the corner and two blocks down from Smiley. Kevin had received Jesus Christ as his personal Savior, as well. He worked at the same Wal-Mart that Smiley worked. They had met each other while they were both sophomores in Germantown High School.

This Sunday morning, Smiley put his head down as the parents stood up and testified about Trigger, the loan shark.

Kevin looked at Smiley and whispered, “It’s a shame that Trigger has you hooked on borrowing from him. You need to stop, man.”

Smiley nudged Kevin and said, “Man, be quiet before somebody hears you.”

After the testimony service was over, Pastor Martin stood up and said, “Parents, keep on praying for your children and Trigger. God says that the day is near, that he’s going to save Trigger and take him out of this neighborhood for a while. Then He will bring him back in this same neighborhood to be of a service to this same neighborhood that he robbed.”

After church service was over, Smiley and Kevin went to Smiley’s house. Ms. Pat was in the kitchen. She was a single parent and raising Smiley the best she knew how. She was happy that Smiley had met Kevin, a nice, respectful, young man that went to church. Even though Ms. Pat was happy her son Smiley went to church, she felt as though she didn't need to go.

As the two young men walked in Smiley's house and entered the kitchen, Ms. Pat said, "Hey Smiley. Hey Kevin. What's going on with you two? How was church today?"

"Mom, prophecy came forth today from Pastor Martin," Smiley told her. "He said the day is near, and that God is going to save Trigger and take him out of this neighborhood for a while. Then He will bring Trigger back to serve this same neighborhood that he has robbed."

"Oh yeah! Well, you two guys just stay away from Trigger. He is not to be trusted."

Smiley and Kevin walked out of the kitchen and went outside to sit on the steps. That's when Smiley began telling Kevin about the dream he kept having.

"Man, I keep having this same dream over and over again. A voice telling me to stop borrowing money from Trigger, or Trigger will shoot and kill me. The voice says there is a better job that I can have that will pay more money than what I'm making now. The voice tells me that I can have it, and then I won't have to borrow money from Trigger no more. The voice says it will make me the lender, not the borrower, and I will be the head and not the tail. It told me to stop borrowing from Trigger, and I will receive the job."

Kevin told him, "Man, why don't you do what the dream is telling you to do, and see what happens. Stop borrowing from Trigger. I heard what your mom said, and I don't trust Trigger either."

"I'm trying to stop borrowing from Trigger, but I can't."

Kevin responded, "Man, you heard the word Pastor Martin preached more than one time. I forget the scripture, but it says something like, the devil comes to kill, steal, and destroy what God has given you. Pastor Martin also said something like, confront the devil and he has to flee. So, all you have to do is tell Trigger that you will pay him all of the money you owe him next week. Then pay him all of his money. Don't tell him you're not going to borrow from him no more. Just don't go back to borrow from him again. It's just that simple, man."

"Yeah, man, I think I'll do that," Smiley told him. "I'm tired of borrowing from the devil. I want to be free."

The two young men got up from off the steps and walked around the corner to go to the store. They hung out for a little while, then said their goodbyes and went home.

Seven months later, Smiley still hadn't paid no attention to his dream or the good advice his best friend had given him. They kept going to church, and life went on as usual. Smiley kept borrowing from Trigger, and he kept owing Trigger.

One Sunday morning, while both young men were walking home from church, they ran into Trigger and Sly as they turned the corner.

Trigger got his name from the gun he carried. In a joking manner, he would say to his clients, "I'll lend you this money, but if you don't pay up, Trigger will get you!" Then he would lift up his shirt to show his gun and let them know he meant what he said. Trigger's best friend was Sly, and he was known as the snitch in the neighborhood.

Trigger walked up to Smiley all high up off drugs. He said to him, “I want my money you owe me today! I don’t want to wait until Friday.”

Little did Smiley know, before Trigger and Sly walked up on them, Trigger had told Sly, “Come on with me, man. I’m going to scare Smiley a little. Watch me play this joke on him. Let’s see how scared he gets.”

“Come on, Trigger, you know I’ll have your money for you Friday. You know I’m good until then,” Smiley said, almost pleading.

“No, you won’t, because you’re not going to be here Friday! You’re not going to owe me money or come short with my money no more.” Trigger pulled out his gun. “Give me my money, Smiley!”

Smiley backed up. “Man, stop playing with that gun before it...”

Before they knew it, the gun went off. Everything happened so fast. What was meant to be a joke turned out to be a tragedy. Trigger’s finger slipped, causing the gun to discharge. Smiley was shot in the chest.

Kevin caught Smiley as he was falling. “Somebody call an ambulance!” Kevin cried out.

Crying and still high, Trigger said, “I’m sorry, Smiley. I didn’t mean to shoot you. I was just playing with you. Tell him, Sly. I just came here to play a joke on you.

Sly stood there speechless and crying, as well.

In the distance, the sound of the ambulance siren could be heard.

Kevin shouted, “Smiley, don’t die on me. I don’t know what I would do without you, man!”

Smiley last words to Kevin were, “I don’t have to borrow from the devil no more. I’m free. Tell Mom I love her.”

Kevin held his best friend in his arms and watched as he took his last breath. While looking up towards the heavens, Kevin hollered out, “Why, God? Why did you let this happen?”

The ambulance soon arrived, and the paramedics put Smiley’s body into the ambulance, quickly starting to working on him as they took him to the hospital, Kevin got in the ambulance with them. While they were trying to resuscitate Smiley, Kevin continued to cry, knowing that Smiley was gone. By the time they got to the hospital, Smiley was pronounced D.O.A. (Dead On Arrival).

Ms. Pat, Smiley's mother, came running up the hall, crying and saying, "Where is he?! Where is my son Smiley? What room is he in?"

The doctor rushed over to her and said, "I'm sorry, but your son arrived here dead on arrival. He's in room three. Again, I'm sorry."

"No, God!" Ms. Pat screamed. "My baby can't be dead! What room is he in?"

As the doctor told her the room number again, she took off running toward room three, while yelling, "Smiley, I'm coming. You're going to be alright."

Clearly, she was in shock and wasn't accepting the fact that Smiley had gone on to be with the Lord. When she got in the room, Kevin was sitting at the bed holding Smiley's hand and crying with his head hanging down.

Ms. Pat ran over to the bed, saying, "Smiley, you're going to be alright. I'm here now." She picked his corpse up in her arms. "I'm going to get you out of here. We're going to go home.

By this time, Kevin had walked over to her. "Ms. Pat, Smiley is gone. He's dead."

Coming to reality, Ms. Pat laid her son's corpse down. Her and Kevin then locked up in a hug and cried.

"Kevin, I can't live without my baby."

"I know, Ms. Pat," Kevin said, trying to console her. "I feel the same way you do. I don't know how I'm going to make it without Smiley."

Just then, Pastor Martin came and grabbed Ms. Pat by the hand. "I'm sorry..."

But before he could say another word, she yanked her hand from his and said, "Don't touch me! It is you and your church's fault that my son is dead."

Ms. Pat was angry with the world. She had to blame somebody for her son's death, so she blamed the church that he went to, saying they should have been there for him so this would not have happened. Before she got to the hospital, Ms. Pat had heard that Trigger was the person who shot her son. What she didn't hear was that it was an accident.

"God tells you everything else. Why didn't he tell you that my son was in trouble?" she asked Pastor Martin.

Knowing that Ms. Pat was angry, Kevin said, "Come on, Ms. Pat, let's talk to the doctor.

"Look at Smiley," she said to Kevin. "He looks like he's just sleeping. I can't believe my Smiley is gone!"

Dr. West came into the room to check on them. "If there is anything I can do for you, let me know and I will assist you in any way that I can," he told the deceased boy's mother.

After thanking the doctor, Ms. Pat sat in the room with Smiley for about twenty minutes. Before they all left the room, her last words were, "I still can't believe my Smiley is gone. He was just here today, and now he's gone. He was a good son."

Ms. Pat kissed her son's corpse, while Kevin rubbed his best friend's hand. Then her and Kevin walked out the room to go talk to Dr. West about arranging where to take Smiley's body.

That evening, Bishop Saul received a phone call from Pastor Martin after he had talked to Kevin and gathered the full story on what led to Smiley's death. He told Bishop Saul all of what happened according to what Smiley's best friend had told him.

Bishop Saul told the pastor, "The neighborhood is in an uproar. They are blaming the church. Smiley's mother is blaming the church because since Smiley had been coming to church faithfully, she felt the church should have been able to see that the young man was in trouble.

She said God shows the church everything else, so why didn't God show us that Smiley was in trouble."

Pastor Martin replied, "Bishop, you can bring a horse to the well, but you can't make him drink. I brought the word of God to Smiley and the church, but I can't make them live it. I have preached many sermons, but God kept putting it on my heart to preach this one sermon every now and again to remind the people to beware of the devil and his tricks. Bishop, you have preached that sermon here, too, more than once."

Bishop Saul ended the call by saying, "I will pray and seek God to see what instructions he will give on how to deal with this matter."

The next day, Bishop Saul pulled up in his new silver Rav-4 Jeep. Confused spirits were in the air. Some neighbors were outside of the church shouting, "Where is the church?" Some people were hanging out their windows shouting, "Where is the church?" Some people were sitting on the church steps shouting, "Where is the church?" Some people were sitting in their cars and some were driving by slowing trying to see and hear what was going on. Some children were sitting on their bikes quietly looking on.

Bishop Saul went inside the church and took Pastor Martin off his knees while he was praying with a few faithful members who were standing in a circle around Pastor Martin. Bishop Saul grabbed the microphone and then took Pastor Martin by his hand as they rushed outside with the few faithful members following behind them.

Bishop Saul began to speak. "Listen every one of you. I am Bishop Saul to those of you who don't know me. Most of you around here know me, and I know you. When I first established The Neighborhood Church of God on this corner of Fifth Avenue, most of you were all broken down in one way or another.

"Some of you were on drugs. You came and got delivered.

Some of you were not saved. You came and got saved.

Some of you were prostitutes. You came and got delivered.

Some of you were sick. You came and got healed.

Some of you were not married. You came, got saved, and then got married.

Some of you were thieves. You came and got delivered.

Some of you were murderers. You came, were forgiven, and got delivered.

Some of you were liars. You came and got delivered.

Some of you were gamblers. You came and got delivered.

Some of you were gossipers. You came and got delivered.

Some of you were homewreckers. You came and got delivered.

Some of you had low self-esteem. You came and got delivered.

Some of you were jobless. God gave you a job.

Some of you didn't have food to eat. You came and received food.

Some of you needed clothes on your back. You came and received clothes.

Some of you were standing in despair and didn't know which way to go. You came and God directed your path.

"Many times, Pastor Martin and I warn you that these times will come, when Satan will come to kill, steal, and destroy what the church has and bring division among you! I hear you from every angle of this neighborhood shouting, 'Where is the church?' You are the church! You got saved and received help inside this church building. You learned God's word, which helped you when you were in the state you were in. Now you ask where is the church when a crisis comes? You leave Pastor Martin and the rest of the church family to come back to the streets.

"Where is the church? You are the church! I'm sorry to hear that Brother Smiley is no longer with us, but he's in a better place. If you're going to stand for what he believed in, he came to church and got saved. If you want to point a finger, point it at yourself! The church or you don't know everything about each other. We all have to help one another any way that we can! If the church knows of any problem that you have, we are here to help you. However, we cannot help you if we don't know that you have a problem. Brother Smiley had a problem that the church was not aware of.

"It's time for us to gather as brothers and sisters in Christ and for the lost of our beloved Brother Smiley. We need to be praying and giving help to his family as well as each other. Don't let Satan rob you of all you have received from God! One day we're going to look for each other, and we too will be gone, hopefully to be with the Lord. We don't know the day or the hour, but just as sure as we are standing here today, we could be gone today. Brother Smiley did what we have to do--live to die. None of us know how, when, or where. We do know that time is winding up. Let us ask God to forgive us and help us in a time such as this.

"Where is the church? You are the church! I am the church! Whosoever will come to receive Jesus as your personal Savior, you will be part of the church. Let us come together with love supporting Smiley's family and supporting each other like Christians and neighbors should do!

"All the word God has been sending to this church through myself and through Pastor Martin, time after time, God would repeat this one sermon through us: Be aware of the devil! In the book of John 10:10, Jesus left us his words of warning to be aware of the devil. The thief cometh not but to steal and to destroy. I come that they might have life and that they might have it more abundantly.

"Jesus left us more of his word in 1-Peter 5:8. The devil will come at times like a roaring lion seeking that he may devour. But, if you resist him, he will flee. If you don't give in to the devil and his tricks, he will leave.

"In the book of Philippians 3:2 and the book of Revelations 22:15, God warns us to be aware of the devil; he will come in many forms. He will come in a dog spirit form at times. Meaning that he will enter people with spirits that are contrary to God, full of wickedness, and bringing division to the church so that God's work and His purpose won't be fulfilled. He will come, but he will be defeated because nobody can stop the will and work of God that is going to be done, one way or another! In this passage, the same spirit I'm telling you about is called a dog spirit, which came in one of Jesus' disciples, Judas. It made him betray Jesus for thirty pieces of silver--Matthew 26:14-15

"Do you people hear what I am saying to you?! You are the church! Don't let no devil come into this neighborhood. This is your neighborhood. Don't let him come and turn you against your church. Don't let him come and turn you against each other. God has brought all of you a mighty long way from where you use to be! He has helped you right here in this church building!

"I think I have said enough," Bishop Saul said. "You understand what I have been telling you. Will there be one that will come down and stand with us in front of your Neighborhood Church Of God? Will there be one that will come, repent, and ask God to forgive you and help you be a support to each other and to Brother Smiley's mother and family?"

Bishop Saul ended with his plea for the people to repent and come together in unity, so that God could help them through this tragedy and help them with their mourning.

People began walking down in front of the church to repent and some to be saved. Trigger and Sly were hiding in the crowd.

As Bishop Saul was speaking, Trigger said to Sly, "The bishop was talking about me, saying the devil dog spirit came in me, made me rob this neighborhood, and made me kill Smiley."

Trigger reached in his pocket for his gun to shoot Bishop Saul, but he couldn't move his hand. He couldn't speak. He couldn't do anything. Then Trigger heard God's voice speak to him.

"No...more...Trigger!"

Unable to speak up, Trigger began whispering to God. "God, if you are real, help me. I want to stop letting the devil use me, but I don't know how to stop him. I want to stop robbing and killing, but this is all I know how to do." Still whispering, he said, "Please help me, God. Please forgive me, God."

Before Trigger knew it, his feet were leading him down in front of the church building. While Bishop Saul spoke, Trigger stood in front of him crying and saying, "I'm sorry! Bishop, help me! I didn't mean to kill Smiley! I was high. I started off playing a joke on him. I didn't mean to kill him. Sly can tell you that I didn't mean to kill Smiley! I want to receive Jesus in my life. I need him to help me. I'm tired of living like this!"

Sly ran down in front of the church. "I want to receive Jesus, too," he said.

That day, Trigger and Sly got saved along with twenty-five other people.

People were in the street crying, some were repenting, and some just stood there witnessing what God was doing through Bishop Saul, who motioned for one of the deacons to come to him. When he came, Bishop Saul whispered in his ear for him to call the police so justice could be done to Trigger. Even though Trigger was about to get saved, he still had to face the consequences of his crime.

Bishop Saul took Trigger by the hand and asked him, "Are you ready for a new beginning in your life?"

"Yes, Bishop," Trigger replied with tears running down his face.

Bishop Saul began reading and explaining Romans 10:9 and Romans 10:13 to Trigger and everyone that was standing in front of the church.

"That if you believe every word in these passages, receive and call on the name of Jesus. Jesus will begin to lead and guide you with his Holy Spirit."

Trigger and everyone that was standing in front of the church got saved. Afterwards, Trigger said, "Okay, Bishop, I'm ready to go do the time for the crime I committed."

By this time, the police who were standing there listening put the cuffs on Trigger's wrists, put him in the police wagon, and pulled off.

Sly ran down in front of the church and said, "Don't forget me, Bishop. I want to get saved. I want a new life like Trigger. He's my best friend!"

"Jesus will be your best friend after you receive him," Bishop Saul told him, then led Sly to Jesus and began praying for everyone in the neighborhood.

From that point on, Sly went to The Neighborhood Church Of God along with the rest of the people that had received Jesus as their personal Savior. The police officers that arrested Trigger and a few of their co-workers also joined The Neighborhood Church Of God. They were drawn by the love of Christ demonstrated to a criminal by this church. The saints became closer than ever to each other; they were in unity and one accord with God.

Six months had passed, and Ms. Pat was still grieving the death of her son. One Sunday morning, Kevin and Ms. Pat walked into The Neighborhood Church Of God. She held on to Kevin's arm as they entered the church. They walked in during the testimonial part of the service. Pastor Martin and the whole church stood up clapping and saying, "Praise the Lord!"

Pastor Martin said, "Praise the Lord. Sister Pat, you are welcome to say a word, if you like."

"Come on and walk with me," Ms. Pat told Kevin.

When they reached the front of the church, Pastor Martin handed the microphone to Ms. Pat.

With tears running down her face, Ms. Pat said, "I'm sorry that I didn't come to church with my son Smiley while he was alive, and I'm sorry I blamed the church for my son's death. I heard that if I want to see my son again, I too must receive Jesus within. Smiley received and loved Jesus. I know he is in heaven smiling, because he always smiled."

Not knowing the order of the church service, Ms. Pat expressed her desire to get saved at that exact moment. "I want to get saved. I want to make sure I get into heaven to see my son Smiley again."

Pastor Martin told her, "We allow the Holy Spirit to have his way anytime he wants to throughout the service. Is there anyone else who wants to receive Jesus in their heart as their personal Savior?"

Six more people approached the altar to get saved. They received Jesus in their hearts, and Pastor Martin prayed for them. The church went up in praise, thanking God for the new souls that got saved. The Holy Spirit calmed everyone down and then brought the word through Pastor Martin. The theme was "After the Storm is Passing Over", Matthew 14:22-32.

After Pastor Martin prayed, gave the benediction, and dismissed the church. Ms. Pat went over to Sly and said, "God has taken my son's life and saved you and Trigger's life. God used my son to draw you, Trigger, and me to him. If God forgave me, I have to forgive you and Trigger. I'm just glad God saved Trigger and you. Now we can have a peaceful neighborhood again."

"Thank you, Ms. Pat, for coming over here to say a word to me," Sly said. "I'm sorry about Smiley. I wish he could be here with me in his church."

Ms. Pat replied, "He see you. He is up in heaven smiling right now. He is always smiling. I'm just glad that one day I will get to see my son again."

"I will get to see him again, too," Sly told her.

They both hugged each other and then departed to head to their destinations. After shaking Sly's hand, Kevin followed Ms. Pat out the door of the church. From that day on, Kevin visited Ms. Pat every day. The bond that he and Smiley shared carried over to him and Miss Pat, as if she was his second mother. Kevin's mother understood it.

Bishop Saul's seventh church, The Neighborhood Church Of God on the corner of Fifth Avenue, was back on one accord with seven hundred members and was still growing with the flow of the Holy Spirit having its way every time the church door opened.

About the Author

Sarah E. Jamison, who received her education in Philadelphia, attended and graduated from the Community College, where she received her license for Kitchen Management. She also went to school for cleaning and received a certificate.

Sarah's mission is serving in the Philadelphia Public Schools.

While secularly working, she works faithfully in the ministry of churches. While attending Bible institutes, she continues spreading the word of God, led by The Holy Spirit and however he leads her.